STEVEN STANDING
In The AFTER

Book 1 of the Steven Standing Series

By RON BRUNK

Steven Standing In The After
Book 1 of the Steven Standing Series

Copyright © 2012 Ron Brunk

ISBN 978-0-9897372-5-8 (ebook)
ISBN 978-0-9897372-6-5 (paperback)

Library of Congress Control Number: 2013917921

Alexia Publishing
PO Box 120942
Nashville, TN 37212
www.alexiapublishing.com
www.ronbrunk.com
ronbrunk@yahoo.com

For You.

You know who you are.

Things are never what they seem

Until the dreamers dream

With eyes wide open

In the Spirit Stream;

Dream cascading down upon dream,

Eyes wide open in the Spirit Stream.

-- Michael Crisp, Spirit Stream, 1976

Chapter 1

Steven Standing had no way of knowing it – even though he was an extremely brilliant boy – but this was not just another day in his life. Steven sat up in bed, rubbed the sleep from his eyes, and stretched his arms over his head. He felt good, *very* good, fully alive and vibrant. In fact, he couldn't remember ever feeling so wonderful.

Steven glanced at the old clock-radio by his bed – the one his grandmother had given him – but there were no little red numbers on the display. He furrowed his brow. *Hhmm, what's up with that?* He pushed its buttons randomly and rapped on the small electronic device to see if it would respond. Static buzzed loudly from the speaker, but the time refused to reappear. *Well, at least it still has power. I'll have to get it checked out later.*

Steven jumped into the shower and as the water burst forth upon him, it seemed as though he'd never felt or smelled or tasted water so fresh and pure. Even brushing his teeth was invigorating. He felt so *alive.*

Later, when Steven emerged from the bathroom, his dog, Bang, was waiting for him by the door, sitting up alert, grinning, his brown eyes dancing with joy at the sight of his master. The dog's father was German shepherd and his mother a prize-winning Blue Heeler, and Bang was a perfectly unique and remarkably intelligent blend of the two strong breeds. He was seventy pounds of exuberance with a black patch of fur on the right side of his face and a white blaze above his left eye.

"There he is! Come here, boy!" Steven said as he sprawled out in the floor and romped with his best friend. The pair tussled about, mock fighting over a shoe, growling and laughing with each other. After several minutes of boisterous play, Steven said, "Hold on, let me catch my breath. We have a big day ahead of us, you know, and I still have to finish getting dressed and ready."

Bang licked his master's face and nuzzled against him while Steven rubbed behind the dog's ears. Bang smiled up at his favorite human, perfectly content, his tongue lolling about.

"Hey, where did you run off to last night, boy?" Steven asked. "It seems like I haven't seen you in, like.... forever."

Steven stopped abruptly and put a hand to his temple. "I don't know what it is, but something just doesn't make sense...I feel weird all of a sudden..."

Bang barked gently a few times and Steven had the odd sensation that he could almost understand what his canine companion was saying. It was as though Bang had said, "Give it time. You'll understand."

Steven rubbed his chin, then stood up and shook himself as if to brush off the strange moment. "Maybe I need something to eat," he said, heading toward the kitchen and remembering leftover pizza in the fridge. Following eagerly at Steven's heel, Bang barked, "Me, too!"

Wide-eyed, Steven stopped in his tracks on the linoleum floor, and spun around toward the dog. "Whoa, wait...what did you say?"

Bang repeated his enthusiastic "Me, too" bark.

"Alright, hold up a minute. I am officially freaking," Steven said, putting his hands out, palms up, in front of himself as if to stop the proceedings. "What in the world is happening here?"

Silence.

Steven began pacing back and forth, back and forth in the kitchen, rubbing his head and mumbling to himself. Bang sat on his haunches by the dining table and watched his master's odd behavior with a smile.

"Okay, now…this is totally creeping me out," Steven continued. "It's like I'm understanding dog talk. How can that be? I must be having a crazy dream. Yeah, that's got to be it…I'm dreaming."

"No, you're not," Bang barked softly.

"Okay, you, just stop talking for a minute."

Bang closed his mouth and hung his head.

Steven went to the kitchen sink and splashed cold water on his face. Then, realizing the absurdity of his action, he said to himself, "I'm guessing water probably isn't going to help, because I just got out of the shower a little while ago. *Unless*…unless I only dreamed that I took a shower. Or maybe…maybe there's something *in* the water. Man, this is making my head spin!"

Steven hurried to the bed and lay back down. "Okay, now, I'm going to be rational about this," he said. "I must have been asleep, caught up in some bizarre dream. But now I'm going to wake up, *for real this time*."

Steven thumped on his chest, slapped his own cheeks, and quickly jumped straight up out of the bed. "Alright, no more dreaming!" he shouted. "I'm totally awake now and everything's back to normal."

There was a knock on the door. Man and dog looked at each other. "Wonder who that is?" Steven said. Bang uttered no reply.

Again came the knock and a woman's voice called out, "Is everything okay in there?"

Steven opened the door and gazed upon a most unusual, yet beautiful woman, probably old enough to be his mother. Her hair was platinum blonde, piled up high on her head, and adorned with flowers and jeweled hair sticks. Her facial features were delicate like those of a china doll, and her eyes were blue and piercing. She wore an elegant gown with a summery floral print, lace and chiffon that flowed behind her like mist in the morning. For a moment, Steven saw nothing else at all, and found that he could not form a coherent sentence.

Bang barked, "Ask her in, dummy." Steven shot the dog a scolding look.

"Hello, my name is Hilda," the woman said, extending her hand. "I heard your dog barking and wanted to make sure everything was okay."

"Yes, yes, I'm okay, I think. I'm sorry if we bothered you." Steven looked at Bang. "He's acting…well, a bit odd today."

Bang barked, "You're acting odd."

Again with the scolding look.

"You know, now that I think about it….maybe I'm not quite well at the moment," Steven said, feeling disoriented again.

"Oh, you poor dear," Hilda said, stepping inside and putting her palm to his forehead. Steven's cheeks turned bright red. "Sometimes the journey does leave one a bit disoriented."

"Yeah, I guess so," Steven mumbled as he slumped into his favorite chair. "Wait…what was that? What journey?"

But Hilda did not hear him. She was already busy in the kitchen, brewing tea and rambling on about a variety of subjects: the weather, the constant influx of new people into the building, choir practice, training classes, and a host of other things. Steven could only catch bits and pieces; mostly he was sitting in a daze, staring at man's best friend, who was staring back at him.

"What are you lookin' at?" Steven grumbled.

No response.

"First you won't shut up; now you have nothing to say. Is that how it's going to be?"

Bang simply sat there panting contentedly, as dogs do, allowing his tongue to hang out one side of his mouth.

Steven said, "Do you know how goofy you look when you do that?"

Still no response.

"You know, if something startled you and caused you to snap your mouth closed, you'd probably bite your tongue in half."

Drolly, Bang murmured, "Just how stupid do you think I am?"

"Here you go," Hilda said coming back into the room. "Drink this tea. It will make you feel better."

She sat down on the sofa and watched Steven sip from the cup. Bang jumped up beside her and Hilda rubbed behind his ears lovingly. He was in heaven.

"It's a beautiful day outside, you know," Hilda said. "When you've finished your tea, we'll go for a walk."

"No offense, but you don't exactly look like you're dressed for a walk," Steven observed.

"What? Oh, this old thing?" Hilda said, lifting and fluffing the train of her dress. "I just threw it on for fun today. Don't you worry, I can get along just fine in it. And as soon as you're ready, let's take that walk. A boy should be outside enjoying himself."

"I'm not a boy; I'm fourteen years old. And if you'd like to know, I'm already taking some college level classes in physics and biology," Steven said proudly.

"Ah, but you are truly forever, don't you know?"

Not at all sure what she meant, Steven studied Hilda for a moment and decided it was pointless to argue with this strange, exotic woman. Instead, he simply stated, "Well, I'm fourteen and I'm also not a nerd, by the way."

"A what?" Hilda asked.

"A nerd, you know, a bookworm. I don't mean to brag, but even though I am at the top of my class academically, I'm also *very* good at sports," Steven said, pointing to the various baseball, football, and other trophies that lined his shelves.

"Yes, as you wish, I'm sure you are."

"My father has a funny saying…or at least, *he* thinks it's funny," Steven grinned. "He always says that a well-*rounded* individual can *roll* with anything. So that's why he always makes sure that I work equally hard on my schoolwork and athletics. He says a person shouldn't put all their eggs in one basket."

"Indeed, it sounds as though your father is wise in the handling of eggs," Hilda said. "Now, drink up and we'll get you some fresh air. Perhaps we'll meet a few of your neighbors."

Meet my neighbors? Steven thought. *I already know all my neighbors.*

To Hilda he spoke haltingly, "Okay…okay…sure." He was still quite confused by the events of the morning, and now the tea was sending a warm, tingly feeling through his body. It felt good, but odd. He stood up and shook himself again, as he had earlier.

"I do appreciate you stopping by, but I really need to finish getting ready," Steven said. "I have a big game today."

"Oh, really? "What kind of game?" Hilda asked.

"Baseball."

"Base…ball?"

"Don't you know what baseball is?"

"I have never heard of it."

"You've got to be kidding! How can someone not know about baseball? It's only the national pastime, the greatest sport ever."

"Well, I'm sure it's a very pleasant thing…"

"*Pleasant?* I guess you really don't know anything about it. Baseball is grass stains and dirt, sweat and guts. It's crushing the ball over the wall. It's ripping your uniform when you slide into home and crash into the catcher in a cloud of dust!"

"Oh, my, that sounds quite awful. Well, you don't have to do any more of that sort of thing here."

"Oh, yes, I do. The playoffs are coming up and I'm the starting shortstop and clean-up batter. My team and my school are depending on me. So I've got to get going…"

"I'm sorry, Steven, but you cannot do your baseball here. Behold, old things have passed away and all things have become new. Let not your heart be troubled; enjoy the peace, harmony and beauty of The After."

Steven narrowed his eyes at the peculiar woman, and turned toward Bang for support. "You know what a baseball is, don't you, boy? I throw the ball and you run and fetch it and bring it back to me all slobbery. You remember that, don't you?"

Bang looked at his master with great compassion, and whined softly and sadly.

"Come on, let's take your mind off the baseball," Hilda said, jumping up. "I'll show you around."

"Show me around? Around *what?* I live here."

"Yes…but you're new here."

"I am not new here. I've lived here for five years."

Hilda caressed Steven's hair in a motherly way. "Ah, poor boy…you have so much to learn."

Chapter 2

Steven Standing and his faithful dog, Bang, followed Hilda as she stepped out the door of the Standing home and directly into a vast apartment complex. Steven was so utterly shocked that he was speechless for a full minute. He looked first at the long corridors stretched out before him, and then back at the front door of his home. He repeated this action several times, rubbed his eyes and shook his head as if it were filled with cobwebs made by drunken spiders.

"Are you alright, my dear?" Hilda asked.

Steven felt sick at his stomach and he put a hand to the wall to steady himself.

"Wh—but—where—where is my front yard?" Steven mumbled. "And the garage and my street and all the neighbors' houses? What's going on here?"

"I'm sorry this is so difficult for you," Hilda said, smiling tenderly at him. "Please try to be patient."

"But…but this is all just so strange. I mean, that was the inside of my house – at least it *looked* like my house – but this is definitely not…something is very wrong…"

Hilda took Steven's hand and said, "Come, sweetie, and walk with me down the stairs."

Numbly and dumbly, Steven did as she asked.

Down, down, down they went, flight after flight after flight of stairs. All along the way, Steven tried hard to pull himself together and devise some sort of plan of action or escape or something or anything at all. Finally, he decided it would be wise to continue a conversation with this strange woman in the hope that she might eventually reveal something helpful.

"We've been walking down stairs for a long while now," Steven said. "Maybe we should have taken an elevator."

"I think the steps are better for you in this particular instance," Hilda said.

"Well, an elevator would have been a lot faster and easier."

"Easy is as easy does," Hilda replied.

"What does that even mean?"

Hilda smiled and kept on walking.

"Did you put something in my tea?" Steven asked. "Did you drug me?"

"Of course not, silly. I simply gave you the standard After-Tea. We all drink it here."

"What is After-Tea? And where is 'here'?"

Hilda shook her head. "My dear boy, you certainly do ask a lot of questions."

"Someone needs a muzzle," Bang yipped with a laugh.

Steven stopped in mid-step, Hilda below him and Bang above him on the stairs. "Ha, ha, very funny," Steven said dryly. "I'm really glad you're both enjoying yourselves and making jokes at my expense. And since I can't get answers from you, and since I can't yet logically reason out what's happened to me, then I'm going to go along with you...for now. We'll all play your stupid little game together."

"That's the spirit!" Hilda said, seemingly oblivious to Steven's sarcasm and displeasure. And down they went to the main floor.

Before she opened the front door, Hilda pulled a pair of dark glasses from her bag. "Here, you might want to put these on."

Confused, Steven stared at the glasses. "Why would I need those?"

"Because it is very bright in The After. Newcomers usually need some time for their eyes to adjust."

Steven considered arguing but then remembered his pledge. "Okay, sure thing, Hilda," he said mockingly. "Of course I'll wear the sunglasses. Whatever you say."

And so, through the door they went and out into the glory of the day. Steven gasped, even with the glasses on, as he stepped out into the world of The After. The sky was the first thing to capture his attention; it was an iridescent aquamarine color so spectacular that it was almost overwhelming.

"Holy wow, this is so completely amazing," Steven whispered breathlessly. After a few minutes, he pulled the dark glasses off and said, "Here…you can have these back…I don't need them."

Transfixed, Steven gazed up into the liquid-like sky, and felt as though he was peering into Eternity. It took tremendous will power for him to eventually tear his eyes away from it in order to survey the rest of his strange, new surroundings.

There was a kaleidoscope of color as far as he could see – lush green lawns, shrubs, and trees spaced between magnificent, ornate skyscrapers – and all of it beyond brilliant, in every hue of infinite possibilities. There were no vehicles of any kind; but there were people, masses of people of every conceivable description, some sitting on benches staring into the amazing sky, some walking in groups and talking happily, and others floating or flying somehow.

Steven rubbed his eyes hard and did a double take, trying to make sense of what he was seeing. Hilda was smiling at him with that same look of motherly compassion that she seemed always to have. But something about her expression made him wonder if perhaps the lights were on in her head but no one was home. So he looked down at Bang. "Do you see that, boy?"

"See what?" Bang said.

"People flying."

"Oh, yes," Bang answered.

"Mm, huh. Okay, sure. Just your average, everyday, flying people, right?" Steven said sarcastically. "Well, why don't we fly too? How about that? Come on, now. Let's fly!" Steven jumped up and down and flapped his arms goofily. "Look at me! I'm flying."

"That is not the way it's done," Hilda said.

"*Oh, I'm sorry.* How foolish of me," Steven mocked, his patience with this game wearing quite thin. "I guess I need to take a flying class. Where can I sign up?"

"Flying classes are in Section F, Building B."

Steven massaged his temples and let out a heavy sigh. "You know, I'm really very tired of all this. I want to know where I am and what is going on. And I want to know right now."

"You are in The After," Hilda said matter-of-factly.

"Okay, lady, I don't mean to be disrespectful, but that's not working for me anymore."

"Perhaps we should go back inside and have some more tea."

"I knew it; there *was* something in that tea, wasn't there?"

"It will make you feel better, calm you down."

"I don't want any more of your lousy tea."

"Now, now…don't upset yourself." Hilda moved toward Steven to embrace and comfort him.

Steven ran.

Bang barked, pleading, "Come back. It's going to be okay."

17

"Let him run for a bit," Hilda said. "Sometimes the transition can be a very difficult thing. I've heard of this sort of thing before."

"I really think I should go with him. He's my master and my best friend," Bang said, starting after Steven.

"No. Stay," Hilda called out. "The poor dear needs some space for now. It's for the best. He'll be back."

From behind Hilda and Bang, a hefty man with a thick, handle-bar moustache and a very deep, gruff voice said, "Maybe not. He might be a mistake, you know. At least, that's what I heard." The man was Mr. Mitchell McGee, a very important representative of the Third Counsel, District 15; and his moustache danced about on his upper lip when he spoke, almost like a skittish squirrel's tail.

"What do you mean 'he might be a mistake'?" Hilda asked.

"Well, don't breathe a word of this to anyone, and you didn't hear it from me, of course; but supposedly there may have been an error in the selection process. It's possible that young man isn't really supposed to be here."

Chapter 3

Steven Standing ran like the wind sweeping down Pajarito Mountain, his legs pumping like powerful pistons. *I've never felt so alive and strong,* he thought. *I feel as though I could run forever.*

He ran past a billion blooming flower bulbs, a million blissful humans, and a thousand towering buildings that reached up into that eerie, ever-present, blue-green atmosphere. Looking down at his feet as he ran, Steven marveled at the streets and paths glowing gold and silver with such mesmerizing splendor. Again, as with the sky, it took all his efforts to pull his eyes away from the hypnotic beauty of the roadway.

Steven noticed a kindly-looking, old man sitting on a bench, and stopped beside him. "Sir, can you help me, please? It may sound ridiculous, but I think…I think maybe I'm lost…or someone has drugged and kidnapped me. I need to speak to a police officer, or whoever is in charge of this crazy place."

The man smiled warmly. "Take it easy, son. You're in no danger here. You'll be just fine in a little while."

"No, no. Don't tell me that," Steven cried. He turned from the man and ran again, even faster than before. He ran until there were no more buildings or people, nothing but gigantic trees and lush foliage that hugged the golden path as it wound through majestic mountains.

Finally, Steven stopped and sat in the crook of a very large rock. He didn't know how long he'd been running or how far he'd come, but he was barely breathing hard and only a little tired. "I must be running on adrenaline," he said to himself in the stillness of the wilderness.

From a tree branch, a raven croaked, "You don't get tired here, you know, or at least not easily. This is what some might call Paradise."

Steven leaped to his feet, shaking, terrified. "What's happening to me? Where am I?"

"I told you. You're in Paradise."

"Shut up! Please, shut up!" Steven screamed.

"Hey, don't blow a fuse, mate. It'll be alright."

"I'm sick and tired of people telling me that it'll be alright."

"Well, I'm not exactly a 'people', now am I?" the bird said with a smile.

Steven paced frantically in a circle, rubbing his hands together, trying to formulate a plan, speaking softly to himself. "Okay, get it together, Steven. You're in some crazy nightmare land where animals talk and people fly and the sky is like the ocean. Maybe I'm in Oz. Yeah, next thing I know there'll probably be flying monkeys."

"Actually, most monkeys can't fly. They can't seem to get the hang of it for some reason," the raven said, casually scratching his head with a wing.

"Listen, you," Steven said, pointing up at the bird. "I asked you to be quiet."

But the raven continued, "I did know one flying monkey a while back, but he was quite the bore. He was so boastful, and always saying things like 'watch this!' and 'can you do a whirly-loop?' and 'look at me now!'. For a bird, as you would imagine, flying is quite the norm and you might say even a bit passé, so I grew weary of his bravado. Now, I have nothing against monkeys per se, of course, but I wasn't a bit disappointed when that particular monkey moved to the jungle on the other side of the city."

Dazed by the diatribe, Steven stared up at the gregarious bird in the tree and asked, "What kind of creature are you? Are you a crow or a raven or a blackbird?"

"Obviously, I am a raven," the bird replied indignantly with slightly ruffled feathers. "In fact, that is my name. You may call me Raven."

"I meant no offense, but I guess I just never paid that much attention to birds before. So it's hard for me to know the difference."

"That's okay. You all look alike to us too." The raven smiled crookedly and hopped to a lower branch. "I bet you expected me to say 'Nevermore', right? I get that all the time."

Steven smiled weakly; he suddenly felt very tired.

"Maybe you should have a sit down," Raven said.

Steven fell back on the rock, closed his eyes, and listened to the sounds of the forest. He hadn't noticed until then, but the woods were full of pleasant animal sounds. The trees were filled with birds of every imaginable type and color, and they were chirping and singing, their voices sometimes in a cacophony of divergent tones, other times blending as one and soaring in a soothing musical chorus.

Steven was nearly asleep when a rustling sound stirred him. He opened his eyes to see a large black bear amble from the brush and sit down directly in front of him. Steven tried to hide his fear, wanting to run but frozen in place, realizing that there was probably no way he could escape the great beast.

"You're going to eat me, aren't you?" Steven asked.

"Why would I do that?"

"Isn't that what bears do with people?"

"Well, actually I've already eaten three humans today, a little girl, her mother, and her grandmother. So I'm going to save you for later."

"Leave him be," the raven called out as he circled above. Then he landed gently on the bear's shoulder.

To Steven the bird said, "He's just making sport; he wouldn't harm a fly, unless provoked, of course."

"That's right, I'm just messin' with ya," the bear said.

The raven whispered in the bear's ear, "The boy's new here."

"Yeah, I kinda' figured that."

Steven stood up suddenly and said, "My phone!" He felt his clothing and checked his pockets, but to no avail. "I must have left it in my room. So much was happening this morning with that woman and my dog, I completely forgot my phone."

"Your what?" Raven asked.

"My cell phone."

"What is a cell phone?"

"You know, for calling people and texting."

"Sorry, not following you," the bear said, scrunching up his nose with a puzzled expression.

Steven shook his head at them. "You can talk but you don't know what a phone is? Jeez, you guys are unbelievable."

"No need for insults," Raven said.

Sitting back down on the rock, Steven began talking to himself again, "If I had my phone I could call my parents, try to explain to them what's going on. I'm sure they could help me get home, help me get out of this crazy madhouse."

"Madhouse?" Raven said. "I ought to peck you in the head."

Steven stood up abruptly. "I've got to go back to the city, that crazy city."

"Why ya gonna do that?" the bear asked. "Don't you like us?"

Steven smiled in spite of himself, in spite of everything that had happened to him, and in spite of the utter absurdity of it all. "Yes, I like you Mr. Bear."

"My name's Nina Nita."

Steven smiled and put a hand to his mouth to stifle a laugh.

"What?" Nina Nita asked.

Steven stammered, "Oh, you see, um, it's just...it's your name. It's a girl's name. Both of them actually."

Nina Nita narrowed his eyes and glared at Steven. "I'm not a girl," he said. "Not that there's anything wrong with that."

"Oh, of course not. It's a fine name," Steven said.

"His name means 'strong bear' in the ancient language," Raven added. "And he certainly is stronger than the average bear."

"Yes, I'm sure the name fits him very well," Steven said, then hesitated, not sure what to say or do next. "Well, okay then...I guess I'd better get going."

"Wait," said Nina Nita. "You didn't tell us your name."

"I am Steven. Steven Standing."

"Standing. Ha," the bear snorted. "And you made fun of *my* name."

"Goodbye," Steven said as he turned onto the path and headed back the way he'd come. "Maybe I'll see you again sometime."

"We'll be watching for you," Raven called out. "Take care, young Steven Standing."

Chapter 4

Steven Standing followed the golden path back the way he'd come, back to the mysterious After City that shimmered and gleamed beneath the aquamarine sky. Everything about the place – city blocks, parks, buildings, shrubbery – was neatly arranged in perfect geometric shapes, evenly spread and distributed as if according to a blueprint of perfection. It gave Steven the impression that someone had gone to great lengths to make this metropolis appear to be the epitome of beauty, and yet, to him it felt very cold, barren and empty of heart and soul.

Steven ran straight to his building where Bang was faithfully waiting for him on the front steps outside. The dog ran to his master when he saw him approaching.

"Hey, boy!" Steven said joyfully, excited to see his best friend again. Bang jumped up and licked Steven's face and the pair tumbled in the grass.

"It's very good to see you," Bang barked. "I was worried that you wouldn't be happy here. I'm so glad you came home."

"Oh, no, this is *not* our home," Steven said as he stood up and brushed off his pants. "And I don't intend to stay here."

"I don't understand," Bang said. "This world is beautiful and peaceful. You have your same old room with all your things, and we can eat and play as much as we want."

"Yes, but where are my parents and Emily? And what about my school and my friends and my team? I've got my whole life ahead of me and things I plan to do."

Dog and master, best friends, looked deeply into each other's eyes for a very long moment. Finally, Bang sighed and said, "I do not understand all the ways and thoughts of humans, but I will be at your side wherever you go, if you'll allow me."

Steven playfully tousled the fur atop Bang's head and said, "Of course, you crazy old dog! That's exactly what I wanted to hear. Now let's hurry inside so that I can get a few things for the journey. We're getting out of here!"

From his room, Steven quickly grabbed some articles of clothing, his baseball gear, and a few other personal items, and stuffed them in his backpack. "Hey, look at my cell phone," he said, holding it up for Bang to see, about to ring his mother's number. "It doesn't show the time, just like the clock radio. That's totally weird."

From behind them, Hilda, standing in the doorway, said, "That's because there is no Time here. I don't mean to intrude. I saw you come home and your door was open."

She sure is snoopy, Steven thought, but to her he said, "That's okay. We're just packing some things for a trip."

"A trip? Why would you wish to take a trip? Everything one could need is right here at home."

"This isn't my home."

"Of course it is," Hilda said, stepping inside and closing the apartment door behind her.

"No, it's not," Steven answered angrily. "Bang and I are going back to our *real* home."

"Oh, my," Hilda said. "But you can't do that, sweetie."

"Well, I'm not staying here," Steven said. "I'd rather go back into the forest and live with the animals I met there."

"No, no...that's no place for a boy. And you must not believe anything those animals tell you down in the Ooljee Forest. They are known to be highly unreliable and sometimes downright deceitful. You cannot trust them."

"Oh, and I can trust *you*?" Steven said.

"Why, yes, of course. I would not lie to you. I will tell you all and everything I know."

"Okay, how did I get here?"

"I do not know," Hilda answered.

"That's what I thought," Steven said. "And exactly where am I? What is this place?"

"Why, this is The After, of course. I've told you that already."

"All of your answers are riddles."

"My answers are as plain as the nose on your face," Hilda said.

"We're leaving," Steven said resolutely. "Come on, boy, let's go."

"Wait, you must speak to the Minister of Relocation first before you can move."

Steven ignored her and headed for the door, but it opened before he could reach it. Standing in the entranceway was a very large man whose long black hair was pulled back into a pony tail that hung to his waist. His forearms were much thicker than Steven's thighs, and his voice rumbled like a train through the room. "I am Mr. Brister, Assistant Minister of Relocation for District 15. You will come with me and we will resolve this matter quickly and efficiently."

Steven's determination was slowed by the strange man's daunting appearance and demeanor, and the room was silent as he looked from Bang to Hilda and back to Brister. Finally, with uncertainty getting the better of him, Steven acquiesced.

Brister led them to the nearby Department of Human Relations, a shiny, silver building that was five stories tall. Each floor was devoted to a particular branch of ministry related to the human population living in District 15. The offices on the first floor dealt with Supply Requests, the second floor with Primary Living Arrangements, the third handled Blessings and Gifts, the fourth was for Planning and Rezoning, and the fifth floor housed two separate Offices: Complaints and Relocation.

The corridors, stairwells, and meeting rooms inside were full of shiny, happy people bustling about and conversing on a wide range of topics. The fifth floor, however, was not so; it was nearly empty in comparison to the others. In fact, Steven's case was the only one to be heard that day in the Relocation Office.

As they passed by the Complaint Office, Steven looked inside. There was apparently only one case there as well – an old man standing before the Minister of Complaint, who sat behind a large, imposing desk. Steven overhead the Minister say, "How many times now have you made this same complaint? A thousand? Ten thousand? Why do you not go and live in peace as your neighbors do?"

The old man's voice was very weak, and Steven, as he moved past the doorway, heard the man reply ever so faintly, "No matter how many times you deny my complaint, I still maintain that I do not belong here."

Mister Brister led Steven, Bang, and Hilda into the Relocation Hearing Office, a sparse room with a desk at the front, a few scattered chairs, and a wooden banister than ran across the middle. The hefty man with the twitchy handlebar moustache, Mr. Mitchell McGee, sat in

27

a back corner and did not make a sound nor move a muscle. A very tall, thin man dressed in a white suit stood behind the desk, waiting for them. His hair also was white as snow, as were his shoes, his tie, and even his skin. In fact, everything about him was pure white, everything but his eyes. They were black as coal at midnight. The very sight of him sent a chill down Steven's spine.

"I am District Minister Volpe," the White Man said. "The two of you will step forward to the center of the testimony circle. The canine must remain behind the banister."

"Pardon me, sir, for inquiring," Hilda said. "I'm just wondering...doesn't Minister Susan typically handle these cases? I was hoping--"

"Minister Susan has been relieved for the day. As Chief Minister of this District, I will hear this particular case myself. These proceedings shall be conducted according to the rules and regulations of The After and by the dictates of Big Father. We shall begin."

Volpe sat down behind the desk and studied Steven and Hilda carefully before beginning the questioning. "So, I understand we have a boy who is a bit confused about his new home."

"Yes, he's a sweet boy who simply needs a little time and guidance," Hilda said. "Perhaps if I can--"

"I would rather hear from the boy," Volpe said, focusing his gaze upon Steven. "What is your name?"

"Steven Standing."

Volpe rubbed his chin and looked out the window. "Hhmmm, Standing, Standing," he repeated, tapping his long white fingernails on his pasty, white cheek. "The name is most odd...somewhat familiar...and not at all pleasant."

Steven shuffled nervously.

"State your desire for relocation," Volpe said sharply.

"Well, I…I'm not sure exactly what you mean, but…"

"Speak up, boy," Volpe said, spitting out the words.

Steven clasped and unclasped his hands, looked down at the floor and then back up. "Well, sir, I simply don't want to stay here."

"You wish a different apartment? Or perhaps to move to a different building? The woman who accompanies you, has she failed in her duties as your Building Overseer?"

"What? No, no. She's fine. It's nothing like that," Steven stammered.

"Well, then, what do you want?"

"I want to go home."

"Home?" Volpe said incredulously. "You are home. You make no sense."

"I just don't understand what's happened to me. This is not the city I live in. Where are my parents and friends? I have a big playoff series this week; I can't let my team down. I've got to get back to where I was before, but I can't figure out how."

"We do not speak of The Before here," Volpe said. "It is completely irrelevant. Nothing of The Before can compare with The After. Behold, old things are passed away and all things have become new."

"Well, that all sounds wonderful, I'm sure, sir," Steven said. "But I just don't belong here. I want to leave."

"Foolishness," Volpe said. "Why would anyone want to leave? This is the place of bliss and glory and contentment. Here in The After, you have nothing to fear ever again. You can live in peace and do as you wish."

"You mean I can do anything I want…"

"That is correct."

"Except leave, you mean."

"Listen, young Standing, I will not tolerate smart-aleck trouble-makers."

"I'm not trying to make trouble; I just want to go home."

"Sir, if I may say one thing, please," Hilda interjected. "With all due respect, it has been suggested that perhaps a slight mistake was made with the boy, a small paperwork error, and that could be--"

Volpe interrupted Hilda, his black eyes steely with barely-contained ferocity, "You are treading dangerously close to blasphemy."

"No, no, sir, I did not mean--"

Volpe pounded on the desk with a mallet. "I have heard all I need to hear in this baseless case for Relocation. Good day."

"But what about my request?" Steven asked.

Volpe ignored Steven and spoke to Hilda, "As Building Overseer, see to it that the boy becomes involved in classes and activities to occupy his mind and facilitate his assimilation into the Society of The After."

"Yes, sir," Hilda said. "He has already expressed an interest in flying. Perhaps we--"

"Yes, yes, good day, now," Volpe said as he stood up and dismissed them. Then to Mister Brister, the monstrous man with the pony tail, he said, "Escort them back to their building. Give the boy some tea and see that he gets some sleep. He'll see things differently when he wakes."

Steven's heart was pounding like a hammer in his chest and his hands were shaking. He wished he could wake up from this crazy nightmare. He wished his parents were here, but he still hadn't had a chance to call or text them since retrieving his phone. And now these strange people were sending him back to that building where he might never have another chance to escape.

"No!" Steven screamed at the top of his lungs. "No, I won't go!"

Steven moved faster than he ever had in his life. With Bang at his side, he leaped over the banister, past Mitchell McGee – who made no attempt whatsoever to stop Steven – and out of the Office in a flash. His escape took Volpe and Brister completely by surprise, but Steven expected they'd soon be in pursuit. There were only two options: go back down the five flights of stairs, or try the door that appeared to lead to the roof.

"Bang, quickly, go down the stairs and out the front. I'll meet you there."

"But what of you? Where are--"

"Just go," Steven shouted. "Run!"

Bang bounded down the stairs while Steven hurried to the roof. Volpe, Brister, and Hilda scrambled from the Hearing Chamber and went immediately down the stairs, not once thinking that Steven would've done otherwise.

The roof was flat and empty and Steven ran to an edge and peered over. It was much too far to jump. He looked for a way to climb down but saw none – no fire escape, nearby trees, power poles, or utility lines of any type. Steven grew frantic as seconds ticked. *Now what?* He looked up into the glowing blue-green sky for an answer. And, suddenly, there it was.

A flying man was floating slowly by, drifting like a feather on the wind. His eyes were half-closed and his hands folded on his chest as if in peaceful, heavenly repose. He was completely unaware of Steven on the roof, only a few feet away.

"Sir, excuse me, sir," Steven said, as loudly as he dared, hoping not to attract the attention of anyone on the ground. "Please, sir, wake up!"

The floating man came out of his trance-like state and smiled blissfully at Steven. "Yessss, young man....how may I help you." His voice was slow and dreamy.

"I...I want to fly with you. May I?"

"Oh, my, I don't know that I can do that," the man replied.

"Yes, yes, you can do it. I know you can," Steven said, trying not to sound panicky. He saw Bang on the ground below, watching him; but Volpe and Brister had not yet made their way down the stairs and through the crowds of people inside the building.

"I don't have time to explain," Steven said. "I'm going to jump. Catch me!"

The man protested, "But I've never carried anyone in flight before--"

Steven leaped off the edge of the building, out into thin air. He struck the hovering man awkwardly and clung to him desperately.

"Oh, my heavens!" the man gasped as he teetered from side to side and strained to maintain his flight. "This is...this is most difficult...and highly unorthodox...I don't know...oh my..."

"Just take me to my building and put me down there. It's not far. Go that way to your right," Steven said, pointing the direction. "Hurry, please! Faster!"

"I'm doing my very best," the man said. "This is all most unusual. Why are you in such a rush?"

Steven thought quickly, not wanting to alarm the man any more than he already had. "It's just that...you see, I'm on a special mission for...for the Minister."

"The Minister? Which Minister?" the man asked.

"The Minister of...Defense," Steven answered, using the first thing that popped into his head.

"I don't believe I've heard of that particular Minister."

"He's top secret and so is my mission. Faster! The Minister will be unhappy with both of us if I don't get there quickly.

"Oh, my, yes, then, we don't want to disappoint the Minister of Defense."

They flew quickly around a corner and out of sight of the Ministry Building, with Bang following on foot. Volpe, Brister and Hilda were nowhere to be seen, and within a few moments they reached Steven's building.

"Put me down here, please," Steven said. The flying man descended, and when they were ten feet from the ground, Steven jumped, rolled, and sprang to his feet. "Thank you, sir," he shouted and waved. "Thank you so much for your help!"

Steven quickly retrieved his backpack from the room while Bang kept watch outside. Fortunately, the Ooljee Forest was in the opposite direction from the Ministry Building where they'd just been, and the pair of escapees raced down the golden road to freedom.

Chapter 5

Steven Standing, with Bang at his side, followed the path of gold back through the forest, running without stopping until he reached the same rock he'd sat on before.

"We'll rest here and I'll call my parents. They'll know what to do," Steven said, taking off his backpack. Leaning back on the large stone, he first dialed his mother's cell and waited. *Come on, Mom, please answer.* But nothing happened – no ringing, no answer, just dead air. He hit the number again but still nothing. He tried his father's cell and Emily's too, but with the same result.

"That's weird," Steven said. "It's showing that I have a strong signal, even out here, but I can't get a call through." He tried calling and texting everyone he could think of but nothing seemed to work. He hung his head and fought back tears.

After a little while, Bang said softly, "Perhaps you should try that emergency number that humans call. I think it's 9-1-1."

Steven smirked at Bang. "Ha, ha. Very funny."

"I wasn't trying to be funny. This *is* an emergency, isn't it?"

Steven thought about that and decided it was worth a try. He hit the numbers and a voice came on the line, a recording that said, "If you're having a difficult time, have some tea and lie down. Remember that all is well in The After. Nothing can harm you here. Give it time…you'll be fine. Give it time…you'll be fine. Give it time…you'll be fine…"

Steven pushed the 'End' button and resisted the temptation to throw his phone into the woods or smash it on the rock in anger. Instead, he kicked the boulder and yelled out in pain.

From above, a voice said, "That wasn't very smart, now was it?"

"Raven, you've come back!" Steven said. "We need your help."

"At your service, young Standing. What can I do for you?"

Steven bit his lip and thought. "Well, do you or Nina Nita know how I can get home?"

Just then, the bear came lumbering out of the woods. Bang, barking and snarling, took a defensive position between his master and the great beast.

Taken aback, Nina Nita stopped and stood up on his hind legs, towering over Steven and Bang. "That's no way to greet somebody."

Bang eyed the bear suspiciously.

"I'm here to help my friend, Steven Standing," Nina Nita said.

"Yes, it's okay, boy. He's on our side," Steven said. "Or at least I think he is."

"Oh, I apologize," Bang said. "Force of habit; sometimes my instincts get the better of me."

"So now, what's this about going home?" Raven asked as he alit on the bear's shoulder, as was often his custom. "I thought your home was in the Great City of The After."

"No, it's not," Steven said. "And I never want to go back to that creepy place again."

"I see," said Raven. "Well, then, where is your home?"

35

"I live at 107 Center Street in Los Alamos, New Mexico."

The bear and the bird stared blankly at Steven.

"That's in the United States of America."

Still blank.

"Hello. Planet Earth, the Milky Way...doesn't any of that ring a bell?" Steven said, exasperated.

Suddenly, a ghostly voice emanated from the dark woods, "He's speaking of The Before." They all turned toward the trees and peered into the gloom where a pair of other-worldly, golden-blue eyes peered back at them.

Bang bristled at the creature in the dark.

"You are Steven Standing?" the voice asked.

"Yes, I am," Steven answered, stepping forward. "Who are you?"

A magnificent She-Wolf appeared from the darkness, moving stealthily and carefully, her ears alert and eyes shining. She was nearly eight feet long, and her coat was a beautiful blend of white, black, brown and gray, with a large diamond-shaped patch of white fur on her forehead. Her markings were more beautiful than any wolf Steven had ever seen in any book, zoo, or television program.

"I am Alexia," the wolf said.

"How did you know my name?" Steven asked.

The She-Wolf smiled and dipped her head slyly. "How could I not know the name of the Mistake who would become the Savior?"

Chapter 6

Steven Standing, Alexia the She-wolf, Raven, Nina Nita the Bear, and Bang the Dog sat by the Eternal Fire in the semi-darkness of the Ooljee Forest. They were well hidden in a maze-like cluster of massive rocks and thick, twisted trees.

"My friends in the forest tell me that there are humans from the City seeking you," Alexia said. "They are searching in a distant part of the wilderness even now, but they will eventually make their way here."

"What should we do?" Steven asked.

"First, there is much you need to learn."

"That's for sure," Steven said. "I have no idea what has happened to me or where I am or what I'm doing here. I mean, the truth is…I'm just a kid who misses his family and is trying to get home. I have a baseball game tonight, and a science project to finish by the end of the week that my father and I are working on together."

"I am sorry, Steven, truly I am," Alexia said softly.

"Earlier back there, you said something about me being a 'savior'…are you sure you don't have me mixed up with another Steven Standing?"

The wolf laughed. "No, I think not. It is your calling; you are the One."

"There are billions of people in the world," Steven protested. "Why is this happening to me?"

"Why *not* you, Steven? We cannot pick and choose the circumstances into which we are cast by the Universe.

The greatest challenge of all is first to learn to embrace your destiny. Only then can you hope to change it."

Steven gazed up at the trees silhouetted against a bright bulbous moon and the cloud wisps whispering against the eerie sky. Finally, he turned back toward the She-Wolf, his eyes moist, and whispered, "If I do as you ask, will I be able to go back home to my family and friends, back to my life?"

"Indeed, it may be the *only* chance you have of ever going back."

Steven nodded. "Then tell me what I need to do."

"I don't have all the answers, but I will explain to you as much as I know," Alexia said. "First you must allow us to teach you the ways of the Ooljee Forest to prepare you for what you may face there. Then you will journey deeper into the wilderness as it bends downward into the Valley of Death where the Black River flows--"

"Oh, come on. You've got to be kidding," Steven interrupted. "Who came up with those names?"

Alexia ignored him and continued, "As I was saying, the Black River flows through the Valley and will lead you across the Nine Meridians to the Chasm of Caves and the Zero Line. There, I have been told, you will find the Portal."

"The Portal?"

"Yes. I have never seen it, but I have heard that it may be the gateway between The Before and The After."

"Everyone here keeps talking about The Before and The After," Steven said. "But no one will tell me exactly what it means."

"It is a very difficult thing," Alexia said.

"All of this is difficult," said Steven.

"Indeed. All I can tell you is that what you knew in The Before does not exist here. You are Now in the land of The After."

"After *what?*" Steven asked.

"After what went Before, of course," Alexia said.

"That's no answer at all," Steven said, greatly exasperated. "You're just talking in circles."

Alexia continued, "I have been told that in The Before, humans attempt to see into the future; they want to know what is ahead for them. As a result, there are all manner of persons – shamans, prophets, fortune tellers, visionaries and the like – who try to gaze into the future and predict what is to come."

"That's true," Steven said. "I had an aunt who claimed to have psychic powers and the ability to see into the future."

"But here in The After, there is no future to view," Alexia said. "There is only the Eternal Now."

"I don't want to look into the future," Steven said. "I want to go back, back to my home, back to the life I had."

Alexia said, "I have heard that there are beings who do have the power to look back at what went before, to peer into the past. These are the Backward Lookers, the Lords of The Before. If you wish to look back, or if you wish to return to The Before – which I am not saying is even possible, though some say it is – then you must seek one of these Backward Lookers."

"But where do I find these people?"

"I have heard they are near the Portal," Alexia said. "But you must understand that some of what I tell you, I have not seen with my own eyes."

Frustrated, Steven stood up and began to pace around the fire, running his hands through his curly, blonde hair. "So, then, if I ever hope to get out of this nightmare, I have to travel through the forest, down to some river, and look for something called a Portal. But for all I know, the entire thing could be some wild goose chase and all for nothing."

Raven rustled his feathers loudly and said, "I knew a wild goose once and she was a constant thorn in--"

Alexia cleared her throat and said politely but firmly, "Raven, perhaps you could save your goose story for later."

"Of course. But this conversation has gone on a bit, you know," Raven said. "I think I'll just go stretch my wings." And off he went into the eerie sky.

Alexia turned her attention back to Steven. "Few have attempted what you wish to do, and only one that I know of has gone and come back to speak of it. But she returned once again to the Lower Places and I have not seen her since."

"She?"

"Yes. She spoke of the Portal though she did not reach it. That is why she went back a second time."

"Did she find it? What happened to her?" Steven asked, feeling a fresh ray of hope.

"I do not know. As I say, I never saw her again."

Steven sunk back down to the ground and stared into the fire. Bang nuzzled against his master to offer comfort.

"Raven was correct," Alexia said. "We have talked enough for now. Let us take some time to rest and refresh ourselves. Then we will resume our conversation, young Steven Standing. I will be in my lair, if you should need me." With that, the great She-Wolf crept through the rocks to her bed.

"You've been awfully quiet tonight, Nina Nita," Steven said. "Cat got your tongue?"

Raven returned and landed on the bear's shoulder. "I knew a cat once that had ten lives. Clerical error, they said."

"A mistake...like me, I guess," Steven said.

"Truth is, the She-Wolf makes me sorta nervous," Nina Nita said in answer to Steven's inquiry. "She's really smart and strong so I keep quiet around her. My mama bear always told me it was best to keep your snout shut and let others think you're a fool, than to open it and prove it."

"Your mother was very wise," Bang said.

Chapter 7

Steven Standing rummaged through his backpack and pulled out a baseball, his lucky bat – nicknamed The Ripper – and two gloves. "While we take a break, I'll show you how to play the national pastime," he said to Raven and Nina Nita. "It's a game called baseball."

"I love games," Nina Nita said. "How do we play?"

"First, put this glove on your, uh, paw...like this," Steven said, slipping his left hand into one of the gloves. The bear tried to do the same but simply could not.

"It doesn't fit," Nina Nita complained. "What is it for?"

"It's for catching the ball. Watch me." Steven threw the baseball high into the air and all eyes watched it soar upward and back down again, where it landed snugly in Steven's glove with a smack. "See?"

"Let me try," Nina Nita said with great excitement. "I bet I can catch it without the glove."

"Sure, here you go," Steven said, handing him the ball.

Nina Nita slung the ball up with all his might, and then, following its trajectory, raced toward where he thought it might land. Looking up at the sky and weaving about on his hind legs, the bear waved his paws awkwardly, waiting for the red-seamed orb to return. "Look at me!" he shouted. "I'm playing the baseball game."

When the ball came down, it smacked him solidly on the snout. Raven fell off his perch laughing. "Ha! Ha!" the bird cawed. "Right on the nose!"

"Ouch," Nina Nita growled. "It's not funny."

"It is from where I'm at," Raven said.

"You just need to practice," Steven said. "You'll be a pro in no time."

Steven retrieved the baseball, tossed it in front of him, and whacked it with the bat. As it soared across the clearing, Steven shouted to Bang, "Get the ball, boy! Go get it!"

The bird and the bear were watching the proceedings with great interest. Bang turned to them, rolled his eyes just a bit, and whispered, "It's a game we used to play in The Before. It makes him happy." With that, Bang raced after the ball, tail wagging excitedly, and returned it, quite slobbery, to Steven Standing.

"Hey, why don't the three of you get out there and shag some flies?" Steven said.

Nina Nita scratched his head. "Shag flies? Uh, not following you."

"Flies," Raven said with disgust. "I don't like flies. Never have. Far be it from me to judge, but they're nasty is what they are. I knew a fly once who never bathed--"

"No, not that kind of fly," Steven said. "I hit the ball and you catch it and throw it back to me."

"Just humor him," Bang said. "Like I do."

"I like baseball," Nina Nita said.

"Yes, you've got a real nose for the game," Raven laughed.

So they spent a pleasant hour shagging flies, and for a little while, even with all the strange and frightening things that had happened to him, Steven had fun playing his favorite game in all the world.

43

Later, when the game was over, they sat again around the Eternal Fire, and Alexia resumed her teaching. "First, young Steven Standing, you must understand that there is great danger in the journey you are soon to take," Alexia said. "If you wish, you are free to walk away from this quest, return to The After, and live in peace."

"Are you trying to scare me out of this?" Steven asked.

"*Are* you scared?"

"No," Steven answered quickly. "Well, okay, maybe a little."

"Good. Fear is natural and it's perfectly normal to experience it. But you must learn to master it."

"How?"

"By embracing it and releasing it."

"What does that mean exactly?"

"You cannot release what you do not hold. So, you must first fully feel the fear and do not try to deny or hide from it. Then, once you take full possession of it, only then can you channel its power to your own purposes."

"I don't know...I'll try to do that..."

"Do you believe with all your heart that you do not belong in The After?"

"Yes, with all my heart," Steven said. "And for the life of me, I don't understand why anyone would ever *want* to stay there."

"For many, both human and otherwise, The After is exactly where they want to be," Alexia countered. "It is a place of contentment, rest, peace, and orderliness."

"Yeah, sure," Steven said dryly. "And they force you to live like cattle or drones, with all your decisions made for you, with no opportunity to choose what you want to do with your life."

"You are young and headstrong," Alexia said. "Realize that there is still much you do not understand.

44

Each individual must make his or her own decision regarding Eternity. For some, contentment is the right choice. It is what they seek, what they need."

"There's a lot more to life than contentment," Steven said indignantly. "And I may be young but I'm not stupid."

"I did not say you were. Far from it. You are a very special young man with extraordinary gifts. I sensed that the moment I met you. I do not know the specifics of your calling, but I know for certain there is a very special purpose for your existence."

"Well, it's nice of you to say those things," Steven said. "But I don't know what makes me so special."

Alexia put her paw up to Steven's chest and said, "What is in here, in your heart, is what makes you. You will discover this as your adventure unfolds."

"Are you going with me and Bang to the Portal?" Steven asked.

Alexia hesitated for a long moment. "I wish I could, but I cannot. I am needed here. I have many pressing responsibilities."

"The bear and I will go with," Raven said with a wink. "We'll keep the boy out of trouble."

"Thank you, Raven," Alexia said. "I was hoping you would volunteer."

"Why, of course!" said Raven.

"Steven Standing is our friend," added Nina Nita.

"When do we leave?" Bang asked.

"First, I must warn you of what you may face," Alexia said. "When you go deeper into the wilderness, some of the creatures there will not be friendly, not at all. There are bloodthirsty packs of wild wolves in the Valley of Death. If you hear their howls, take to the trees to save yourselves."

"Surely they are relatives of yours," Raven said. "Couldn't you send them a friendly message to leave us be, to let us pass through in peace?"

"They are not like me; their spirits are twisted," Alexia said. "Like most creatures in the valley, they drink from the Black River. Those waters poison the soul. You must not drink from that river, under any circumstances. And if you must enter the water, do not spend long there."

"Okay, so if we see those wolves, we should climb into the trees where they can't reach us, right?" Steven said.

"Yes, but be very careful," Alexia said. "Beware of the tree snakes."

"Tree snakes?" Bang asked. "I don't like snakes of any type – tree or otherwise."

"These snakes hang from the tree limbs like branches or vines," Alexia continued. "They blend into their surroundings so that they may prey upon their victims."

"I suppose they eat small creatures," Steven said hopefully. "Like chipmunks and sparrows and--"

"They will eat anything," Alexia warned. "Fortunately, their poison is not typically powerful enough to kill creatures as large as you...unless you're bitten several times, of course."

"Well, that's some consolation," Steven said.

"The poison of the tree frogs, however, is another matter entirely," Alexia continued. "One bite, depending on the venom of the frog, may paralyze you within moments."

No one said anything for a while, as they were all deep in thought, and the only sound was the crackling of the fire.

Finally, Steven said, "Maybe the trees aren't such a good idea. Maybe we should just take our chances with the wolves on the ground."

Alexia smiled and licked Steven's cheek, as he sat with his chin resting on folded hands on the handle end of his Louisville Slugger. She said, "You are not alone and you are not without powers, young Steven Standing. Hold your weapon out into the Eternal Fire."

"Weapon? You mean my bat? No way," Steven protested, clutching the bat to his chest. "It's made of wood; it'll burn up."

"Trust me. It will not burn."

"This is my lucky bat, you know. I hit .678 this season with it," Steven said wistfully, rubbing his hands along the scuffed wood. "Led the league in homers too. Coach says I could get a baseball scholarship easy."

"Hold the bat in the fire," Alexia repeated sternly.

"Okay, okay," Steven said, moving The Ripper hesitantly toward the flames. "This is crazy, you know." Finally, Steven took a deep breath and thrust the bat into the fire.

It did not burn but it began to glow, first a brilliant blue, then a blazing white. Alexia lifted her head and howled mournfully, yet joyously, at the giant moon above them. Steven's skin crawled on his arms and Bang's fur stood up on his neck.

Alexia ceased her howl and said, "You can take it out now. It has been kissed and empowered by the Eternal Fire."

"What does that mean?" Steven asked.

"It means that when the time comes, you will hit more...*homers* than you ever imagined."

"Cool," Steven said, wide-eyed. He stood and positioned himself in a batter's stance, tapped the bat against the insoles of his feet, studied the pitcher in the eye of his mind, and swung with perfect form, sending an imaginary fastball sailing over the center field wall. "Yeah, man, it feels good, really good."

"Come with me," Alexia said. "All of you."

They walked a ways into the wilderness and stopped in front of a strange, yellowish plant. It had thick leaf pads like a prickly-pear cactus and long stalks with tiny orange flowers like a hobblebush.

"This is the Succato plant," Alexia said.

"It looks like some kind of weird mutant plant," Steven observed.

"Break open the green leaf pads and drink the milk of the Succato, and for a time, it will give you power over the plant life around you," Alexia said.

"Why would I want that?"

"Trust me. Remember what I tell you and in your time of need, it may save you. Furthermore, chew the dirt around the roots of the Succato plant and--"

"You expect me to *eat dirt*?"

Alexia gave him a scolding look and continued, "Eat the dirt around the roots of the plant and it will give you power over the soil itself. Remember what I say."

"Okay, okay," Steven said. "Drink the milk, eat the dirt. I got it."

"But it must be the Succato plant. Study it closely so that you remember it. If you drink from the wrong plant…" Alexia's voice trailed off as she turned back toward the fire. Steven followed close behind. "What? If I drink the wrong plant, what?"

"Just be sure it's the Succato," Alexia said. "Now I must also warn you about a potential enemy. He is a human of great authority in The After. He may not yet be aware of you, but if he does learn that you fled the Great City, he will likely become involved. Trust me, there are great powers at work in this matter, and whatever you do, you should do quickly, young Steven Standing."

"Who is this man, this enemy?"

"He is the White Man," Alexia answered. "His clothes, hair, skin, everything about him is white as snow. All but his eyes."

"Volpe," Steven said, with jaws clenched. "He must be the White Man you're talking about."

"Yes, that is what humans call him," Alexia said. "He is a high-ranking member of the Order of the Letter Of The Law, a pharisaic-like group devoted to the most primitive teachings of Big Father. They have been growing in numbers and power in The After. How do you know of the White Man?"

"He conducted my hearing. He ordered us back to our building, but we escaped and came here."

Alexia growled deep in her throat and paced before the fire. "This is not good. You must prepare yourselves quickly and go."

"Wait a minute," Steven protested. "The White Man? Big Father? The Order of the Letter of what? You can't just throw all that out there at me and then not explain."

"There is no time for that," Alexia said as she sidled closer to Steven. Her long, beautiful coat of dark colors shimmered in the bright moonlight, and the white diamond upon her forehead seemed to glow as she peered into his eyes. "But I give you these final words of wisdom: Steven Standing, you are a tender, kind soul, but you must also be prepared for rage. There is most certainly a time to be clever, but also a time to stand and fight. Know the difference."

Steven nodded and trembled as a stiff breeze whipped the flames of the Eternal Fire.

Baring her sharp teeth, Alexia bristled, "And when the time comes, do not be afraid to show your fangs."

Chapter 8

Steven Standing was troubled but hopeful as he, Bang, Nina Nita and Raven set out on their journey. The four of them moved quickly at first, often at a run, and traveled for days, plunging ever more deeply into the Ooljee Forest and farther from The After and their pursuers. Or so they hoped.

No matter how hard he tried, Steven couldn't stop thinking about his parents and his old life in The Before. He wondered how his friends and his baseball team were doing. He wondered if Volpe, the White Man, was close behind on the trail, coming for him. And of course, he thought about the dangers that might be lurking ahead in the wilderness.

Soon, the vegetation grew increasingly thick, wild, and jungle-like as they began the long, slow descent into the Valley of Death. Long vines hung in bunches from the massive trees that nearly blocked out the sky; and the ground was full of long-needled ferns, black flowers, and an unimaginable number of other exotic plants. Even the air seemed to become thicker, oppressive and ominous, with great patches of dense fog and swirling mist. From time to time, Steven had the unnerving feeling that he and his companions were being watched, and he sometimes caught glimpses of bizarre creatures – a blur of movement here, a flash of something there – but couldn't quite make out what they were.

Darkness took the sky and threw down a cold rain upon the four travelers. Lightning danced from cloud to cloud and thunder shook the ground.

"What is this?" Nina Nita asked. "What's happening?"

"It's called a thunderstorm," Steven answered. "And it's a very bad one."

"I don't like it, not one little bit," Nina Nita said. "We don't have thunderstorms in our part of the forest. Maybe we should go back."

"We're not going back. It's just a little water and clouds moving about," Raven said. "I saw one of these before, from above, once when I was flying rather high. It's quite lovely from up there."

"Well, it's ugly down here," Nina Nita said, and he began to growl and roar at the elements.

"That won't do any good, you silly bear," Raven cawed, landing upon his shoulder. "You need to relax."

"Maybe we should find shelter of some type," Steven said. "And keep warm until this passes."

"Friends, it's doing no good to stand here and discuss it in the rain," Bang barked. "Let's keep moving and maybe we'll find a cave or something along the way."

"I like caves," Nina Nita said.

"There are usually bats in caves," said Raven. "I don't like bats. I once shared a branch with one and his personality was abrasive, his breath atrocious, and he squeaked and squealed all hours of the night."

In a little while they found a cave, just large enough for the four of them to hide, though Nina Nita was barely able to fit through the entranceway. They lay side by side in the small grotto and listened to the wind, rain and thunder roaring outside.

Steven rubbed lovingly behind Bang's ears and said, "I wonder why Alexia didn't come with us. I really

51

thought she would, and I'd feel a lot better about all of this if she had."

"She's the boss of the Forest," Nina Nita said. "She's very busy."

"I'm afraid that's not entirely the reason," Raven said. "I heard that if Alexia comes here, she will die."

"Why?" Steven asked.

"Long ago, she resisted the Great Serpent and he decreed that he would destroy her if she ever again set paw in his part of the Ooljee."

"The Great Serpent? What or who is that?"

"He's the worst, most evil creature in all the world," Nina Nita said. "I don't like him. Nobody does."

"Some do," Raven corrected. "Perhaps many do."

Steven sat up abruptly in the small cave and bumped his head on the rock overhead. "Ouch!" he shouted angrily, and fell back onto his elbows in the dirt. "The worst, most evil creature in the world? Why didn't Alexia say anything about him?"

It was silent inside the cave for a moment. Finally, Nina Nita said, "Maybe she forgot."

"She probably figured you had enough to worry about," Raven suggested.

Steven lay back down and rubbed the bump on his head, "Let's not talk about it anymore right now, okay? Let's just rest for a while."

Bang nuzzled close to comfort his master in the darkness and said, "Don't worry. We'll get through this together. I promise we will."

Chapter 9

Steven Standing crawled from their hideaway after the storm passed, out into a soaking wet world where day was breaking. Sunlight filtered through the leaves and sparkled on rainwater pooled in the dark soil.

"It's so beautiful it almost makes me forget what a dangerous place this is," Steven said as they surveyed the scene.

"Don't forget the bag," Raven called to Nina Nita. The bear tugged the rucksack from the cave and hoisted it onto his broad back as though it were a bag of marshmallows.

"We'd best get going," Raven said. "There won't be much daylight."

"I noticed that the sun seems to shine only briefly, less and less every day," Steven said. "Why is that?"

"Because the further one goes into the Ooljee Forest, the more the Moon takes control of the sky," Raven answered. "The deeper we go into it, the shorter will be the daylight, until finally, only darkness. But I have heard tales of a sunny, blue sky with white clouds beyond the Chasm."

"Well, then, yes. Let's definitely get going," Steven said. "It would be great to see a normal sky again, like back home."

They struck off into the wilderness once more at a rapid pace, over ridges, across streams, down through rugged ravines, and always fighting against the thick undergrowth. The golden road that Steven had first followed away from the After City had gradually turned into a path in the forest; and now as they grew closer to the Valley of Death, that path was dwindling quickly into a barely discernible trail. As the light of day faded, they pushed on through dense brush where it seemed as though no one had ever walked before.

"Did we take a wrong turn and lose the path somewhere?" Steven asked

"I don't think so," Bang said. "I lost any scent of a trail far back, at least of any man or beast with which I am familiar. I believe we are in uncharted territory."

Raven said, "I'll take a look see," and he weaved his way up and out of the thick canopy of trees to scout from above. Returning, he said, "I can't spot a trail of any type from up there."

"I can make a trail," Nina Nita said. The bear lumbered headfirst into the thicket and shouted, "Follow me!"

And so they did.

With Raven perched upon the pack on his back, Nina Nita cleared the way, tromping down plants and pushing aside branches. Occasionally an errant limb snapped back and popped Steven across the chest, but otherwise, the four journeyed on without incident until the darkness settled in and the bear could barely see twelve inches in front of his snout. The great moon was above them but much of its luminosity was blocked by the thick crush of trees.

"I have an idea; I can use my bat to clear the way," Steven said, as they stopped to rest on a rock.

When he pulled The Ripper from his backpack, it began to glow, radiating a soft white light. "Hey, check it out!" Steven shouted. "How cool is this!"

"Ah, yes, remember that the power of the Eternal Fire burns within it," Raven said.

"Yeah, awesome. Well, alright, then let's go," Steven said with fresh enthusiasm. "I'll lead the way with The Ripper."

Their descent into the valley had been gradual at first, almost imperceptible, but soon the grade steepened and they were traveling downhill at an ever-increasing slant. The trees were massive in height and circumference, with huge gnarly roots that jutted out from the ground and twisted about. And there were new sounds in the forest – the strange calls, growls and chatter of unknown creatures in the branches above them and in the thicket around them.

"Sure wish the daylight would come again," Steven said, swinging The Ripper from side to side, knocking down plants and shining the soft light ahead.

They came upon another small clearing and stopped to gather themselves. "My arm is tired from swinging the bat. Let's take a break," Steven said, sitting down hard upon a log.

"It feels a bit safer here in this open spot, even if it's not very big," Raven said. "I like knowing I can spread my wings if I have to."

Once again, Steven tried calling and texting his parents and friends, but with no success. "I just don't understand why none of my calls will go through. I have full signal but can't access email, get online or do anything at all."

Bang was staring into the woods, focused intently on the area where they'd just been. The hair on his neck stood up and he growled quietly, deep in his throat.

"What is it, boy?"

"There's something in there," Bang whispered.

Steven peered into the thicket in the pale moonlight. "Where? I don't see anything."

"There, just to the left," Bang pointed with his snout. "And there. And over there."

"Yes, I see them too," Raven said. "And I hear them breathing. Birds can hear very well, you know."

Steven squinted and studied the brush carefully, desperately wanting to see what his friends saw. Sinister shadows shifted ever so slightly as branches and leaves swayed in the cool, night wind. Fingers of fog reached through the forest, creeping toward them. And then suddenly Steven saw it – a pair of crimson eyes looking back at him. And then another pair, and another, just as Bang had said. Soon, it was a circle of eyes in the wall of darkness. The hair on Steven's arms stood on end.

"Uh, oh," Steven said, his voice barely a whisper. "What do you think they are?"

Bang sniffed the air and said, "Wolves."

Chapter 10

Steven Standing gripped The Ripper tightly with both hands and rose cautiously to his feet. He counted at least ten pair of red eyes watching him from the darkness, locked onto his every move.

"I wonder what they're doing," Steven said.

"I suspect they are assessing us," Raven said. "It could be that we are merely a curiosity to them."

"Well, they're not howling," Nina Nita said. "Alexia said we should climb a tree if they howled. Remember?"

"He's right," Bang said. "They may not be a real threat to us. They could be as scared of us as we are of them."

"Or maybe they're just not hungry right now," Steven said. "I think we should keep moving along casually. Don't let them know you're afraid."

"I'm not scared of any old wolf," Nina Nita said. "Well, except for Alexia."

"Stick close together and guard each other's backs," Steven said. "Keep moving, but don't run. They might take that as a sign of fear and decide to attack us."

The four travelers resumed their journey through the forest, descending toward the bottom of the Valley of Death where they hoped to find the Black River. The wolves followed like specters dancing in the shadows around them, well concealed but always close enough to bring a shudder.

After many miles, the sky began to brighten and the landscape changed. There was more open space, the trees were farther apart, and the undergrowth more sparse. Limestone outcroppings appeared here and there, and the forest floor became a soft bed of pine needles, ferns and moss.

"Now that we have some daylight," Steven said. "We should use it to our advantage."

"You mean stop and rest?" Nina Nita grunted.

"No, absolutely not," Steven replied. "The wolves seem to be gone. Now we can run and really cover some ground. Come on!" Steven sprinted off through the forest with Bang at his side.

"But I'm tired," the bear grumbled, lagging behind.

"Stop your complaining," Raven said. "You're not tired. I've seen you work for days on end just to steal honey from a beehive."

"That's different," Nina Nita said. "I'll do anything for honey."

"Don't forget that our friend, Steven Standing, needs us," Raven said. "We promised the She-Wolf that we'd take care of him. You don't want to make her angry, do you?"

Nina Nita quickened his pace.

Soon the sky began to blacken once again and the thick fog came creeping in. The band of four paused at the mouth of a narrow ravine.

"Think the wolves will be back?" Steven asked.

"Maybe they lost interest in us," Bang suggested.

"Wishful thinking," Raven said, fluttering his wings from his perch upon the backpack. "I think the three of you should hurry through this ravine while I fly overhead as lookout."

"Good idea," Steven said. "Let's go."

The passageway was narrow, only ten feet across at its widest point and three feet at its most narrow, and sloped downhill at a slight angle. The sides were steep and rocky, rising up twenty feet on both sides. Footing was difficult for them as they stumbled over loose rocks and scattered clumps of prickly weeds and thorny brush.

There were few trees along the top edges of the ravine, so the moon was now fully visible, huge and bright above them, overwhelming the sky. It was eerily quiet in the gully, with only the sound of their breathing and their footsteps in the detritus. No one said a word as they raced on, plunging ever deeper into the Valley of Death, ever closer to the Black River, and ever nearer to the Unknown waiting ahead.

The first howl was far away and it drifted on the air like a mournful wail, calling across the ages. Steven, Bang and Nina Nita stopped abruptly and listened. Overhead, Raven cawed, "I don't see anything yet. That was a long way off."

Then came a second howl and it sounded closer; still off in the distance, but closer, nonetheless. Once again Steven felt the hair on his arms stand up.

"Let's move," Steven said with urgency in his voice. "Let's put as much distance between us and them as we can." He gripped his bat tightly and ran like the wind, doing his best to beat down the fear that was threatening to rise up within him and take control.

Soon the howls were cascading, mixed with yelps and guttural snarls, growing louder and closer each moment. The wolves were gaining on them.

Raven swooped down close to Steven and flew beside him at eye level. "They've caught up with us!" the bird screeched. "They're running along the edges of the ravine above."

Suddenly the passageway opened up into a wider, circular clearing, nearly thirty feet in diameter. Steven, Bang, and Nina Nita stood in the center, breathing hard, backs pressed together in a defensive posture, looking up at the pack of wolves now lining the rim of the ravine all around and above them.

The wolves fell silent as the largest one, the leader of the pack, gazed down with a chilling calm at the four trapped travelers. He sat on his haunches, head up, nostrils twitching, and pointed his nose toward the moon. His cry was sad and wicked, beautiful and terrifying. The rest of the pack joined in the song, raising an ear-splitting cacophony that chilled Steven Standing to the bone.

"Where's a tree when you need one?" Steven whispered.

The wolves leaped down one by one into the ravine. They were fearsome creatures with ragged coats and gaunt bodies fueled by hunger, rage and desperation; and they circled slowly, drawing closer, surrounding their prey, preparing for the moment of attack. Their steely, red eyes burned with bloodlust, and they gnashed their teeth and foamed at the mouth.

"I think they're hungry now," Nina Nita said.

"Bang, my friend, I must disagree with your earlier comment," Raven said. "I don't think they're as scared of us as we are of them."

Steven clutched The Ripper with both hands, pointed the bat toward the leader of the pack, and waved it slowly back and forth in a threatening manner. His throat felt like it was full of sand and he swallowed hard, doing his best to remain calm.

Bang was snarling with barely controlled rage while Nina Nita made an intimidating figure, standing tall on his hind legs and roaring. No one noticed Raven circling high overhead.

Several of the wolves rushed forward at once, leaping toward their prey, baring white fangs to the roots. Steven swung The Ripper with all his might and clubbed one of the beasts in the head, sending it sprawling lifeless to the ground with a thud. As Steven turned, another wolf slashed at his shoulder, tearing the flesh, bringing blood. Nina Nita grabbed the attacker and bit into its neck, ripping its jugular vein. "Nobody hurts my friend!" he roared.

Other wolves attacked the bear simultaneously, snapping at his hind legs from all sides. Nina Nita swung his paws wildly at them, his great claws extended, gashing and slicing into their bodies.

Bang was smaller than the wolves, but faster and more agile. He fought tooth and nail, darting among them with quick slashing attacks, ripping into their shoulders and necks. But he took a beating in the process; his ears were shredded and his body tattered with bite marks and blood.

When Bang attempted to retreat to his master's side, one of the wolves bit into his left hind leg and held on. Bang yelped in pain and tried to turn on his attacker, but the wolf evaded him while maintaining its grip. Bang knew that he had to escape quickly or the wolf would crush through the bone, disabling him.

Suddenly, Raven slammed into the wolf's head like a cannonball shot from above. The bird screeched like a creature from another world, stabbed his beak into the eye of the wolf, and ripped it from its socket. Another wolf immediately leaped upon Raven and held him to the ground with his paws. The wicked creature smiled and drooled, but before he could devour the helpless bird, the sweet spot of Steven's bat connected with the wolf's skull and crushed it.

For a moment there was a lull in the combat. The wolf pack drew back a short distance to gather itself and prepare for another assault.

Steven Standing surveyed the bloody scene. He counted six dead wolves, four badly wounded ones, and almost thirty others still ready to fight. Steven's shoulder and thigh had been bitten in the struggle and they were throbbing now. Bang, Nina Nita and Raven were also bloodied and exhausted.

"Things aren't looking too good," Steven said as he watched the slinking beasts. "There are just so many of them."

"That's not the sort of thing a captain should say to his troops, you know," said Raven. "Not very inspiring."

"I'm sorry," Steven said. "You're right." He stared hard at the pack of wolves and shouted at them, "That the best you got? Come on, bring it. We're not afraid!"

"I didn't mean you should antagonize them," Raven squawked. "I was simply suggesting we keep a positive attitude."

Growling viciously deep in their throats, the pack moved forward slowly this time, with a sort of confident swagger to their step, as if they already knew for certain the outcome of the battle.

"I don't like how they're looking at us," Nina Nita said.

The pack surged upon them at once, suddenly and violently, knocking Steven to the ground. Immediately, Nina Nita positioned himself over top of Steven, with a huge, furry leg on either side, straddling Steven to protect him from the wolves as they tried to get at the young man.

The pack shifted their attention to the bear, thinking that if they took him down, the others would be easy prey. Some leaped upon Nina Nita and sunk their teeth into his back. Others, darting in and out, snapped at his legs and hind quarters. But Nina Nita refused to go down.

With Bang close at his side, Steven struggled to his feet, swinging The Ripper wildly back and forth, up and down in desperation. Sometimes he connected with one of the attackers, but often he caught only air. He was tired and didn't know how much longer he could last.

62

Suddenly there was terrifying roar of fury and a flash of white as a vengeful creature landed in the midst of the pack. Steven wasn't sure what was happening and in the semi-darkness it was hard to tell. All he knew was that the wolves appeared to have a new foe attacking them from the rear. The battle grew more brutal and violent as the newcomer tore into the wolves with a wild leap and snarl. There was flashing and slashing of savage teeth, fur and blood flying beneath the huge moon.

"What's going on?" Steven asked.

From above, Raven shouted, "It's Alexia! She needs our help. Quickly!"

His Louisville Slugger was shimmering with energy, glowing bright white as Steven tore into the wolves with frenzied rage. Through the crush of animals, he saw Alexia and they locked eyes. She was fighting for her life, for *his* life.

"Steven! You must go! Now!" Alexia roared through the din.

"No! We're not going to leave you here," Steven shouted.

"There is no time to argue," Alexia said as she fought off attackers on every side. "These wolves want me even more than they want you. We have a history. I can distract them."

"No, I won't leave you," Steven said.

With her mane bristling in the moonlight and blood pooling around her, Alexia growled at Steven, "Volpe is coming to destroy you."

The world seemed to stand still for the slightest of moments and Steven felt suddenly very tired. His brain was swirling. *Why is all of this happening to me? What am I doing here? I want out of this nightmare. I just want to go home.*

"Steven Standing! You must live," Alexia shouted. "I will sacrifice myself for you, if need be. Remember everything I told you. Now go quickly!"

Steven felt himself being lifted up into the air. It was Nina Nita picking him and placing him on his shoulders where the wolves could not reach him. Faintly, he heard Alexia say, "The Ripper has more power than you yet know. Use it. Believe in yourself."

Focused on the great She-Wolf, long the object of their hatred, the pack paid little attention as Nina Nita, Bang and Raven escaped with young Steven Standing.

Chapter 11

Steven Standing woke to the pleasant sound of water lapping gently on a nearby shore. He lay on his back in the grass and stared up at the sun peeking through the trees overhead. The lush smell of fresh clover was strong in his nostrils, and he inhaled and exhaled deeply, slowly. It was a dream-like moment and Steven couldn't quite get his bearings, couldn't quite remember where he was, or why, or how. Somewhere in the back of his brain he heard someone or some*thing* murmur the word *Drink*.

He sat up suddenly, straight as an arrow, and gasped, "Alexia!"

Bang ran to Steven's side and nuzzled him. "It's okay. You're safe now."

"What...what happened?" Steven asked, still a bit disoriented. He put a hand up to his left shoulder and groaned, suddenly cognizant of the pain there.

"The bad wolves bit you there," Nina Nita said. "But Raven told me how to make a poultice of plants and mud. I put it on you myself. You're gonna be okay, my good friend, Steven Standing."

Drink.

"And you did a very fine job of tending to the wound...for a clumsy bear, that is," Raven said, smiling and winking at his friend.

"Thank you for taking care of me," Steven said, standing up gingerly and looking around. "Where are we?"

"The Black River," Bang replied. "We ran for a long time after escaping the wolves, and we stopped here to rest just a little while ago."

Drink.

"What about Alexia?" Steven asked.

Bang shook his head sadly. "I don't know."

"I bet she got away and went home," Nina Nita said.

"Perhaps," Raven said.

"I *know* she got away," Nita Nina said, like a child who very much wants to believe something to be true.

"Yes, my old friend, she probably did," Raven said.

Drink.

Two deer – a fawn and its mother – stepped out of the trees and walked directly through their midst, as if the four travelers weren't even there. The deer went straight to the riverbank, dipped their heads to the water, and began to drink.

"What was that all about?" Steven asked.

"Most curious," Raven said.

"Look," Bang barked. "More animals are coming."

Moose, coyotes, birds, squirrels, raccoons, foxes and scores of other creatures were trickling out of the forest, all up and down the riverbank, and heading for the dark water.

Drink.

"I'm feeling very thirsty, too," Nina Nita said, starting toward the river. "I've really got to have some of that water."

"No, wait!" Steven shouted. "Don't you remember what Alexia said? We must not drink from the Black River."

"It'll be okay," Nina Nita said. "I'm real thirsty."

"Steven's right," Raven squawked. "Stay away from it!"

Drink.

66

As if in a trance,/ Bang also started toward the water, and Steven felt a powerful urge to drink as well.

Drink.

Drink.

Just then, the two deer turned from the river, having drunk their fill, and hissed at the four travelers. Their eyes were burning red and they pawed the dirt threateningly with their hooves.

"What's happened to them?" Steven asked.

The mother deer charged and rammed into Nina Nita.

"Hey, you clumsy deer!" the bear shouted. "Watch where you're going."

The attack of the deer temporarily broke the spell of the mysterious river, and Steven shook the cobwebs out of his head. "Did you guys hear a voice in your mind saying, 'Drink'?"

"I heard it," Nina Nita said. Bang and Raven affirmed that they too had heard the ghostly command.

"I think we should get out of here fast," Steven said.

"Yes, the water seems to make the animals violent and aggressive," Raven added. "We'd best move on before they all attack us."

Suddenly a loud voice boomed from above, "Young Standing has much more pressing matters about which to be concerned!" The four travelers looked up to see the dreaded Minister Volpe descending from the sky on the back of a winged, white stallion.

The animals fled back to the forest, scattering in fear at the sight of The White Man coming in power and glory. Steven and his companions stood their ground as the steed landed on the riverbank, its great wings stirring up masses of dust and leaves, its massive hooves thudding heavily into the dirt.

"I have come for you, Standing," the White Man said. "You will return to the After City with me."

"I won't go back there," Steven said defiantly.

"Oh, but you will," Volpe said with a wicked smile. "I underestimated you before, but I will not do so again. You are the property of The After and I am here to retrieve you. No one defies the Will of Big Father."

Barking and snarling ferociously, Bang stood between his master and the man on the horse. Volpe looked upon Bang as a creature not even worthy of his time or consideration. "Silence your mutt," Volpe said to Steven. "Or I will do it for you."

"Leave him alone," Steven said as Bang barked even more viciously. "He's my best friend and he's just trying to protect me."

Volpe laughed and said with a sneer, "Protect you? You must be joking, young Standing." He then pointed at Bang and bellowed, "Canine, be silent, Xaudium!" and the dog immediately lost his voice. Bang continued to open his mouth, to move his throat and tongue, but no sound came forth from his lips. In anger, the faithful dog leaped forward, gnashing his teeth and snapping at the man on the horse, but the steed danced away.

Pointing at a gnarly vine on a nearby tree, Volpe said, "Xtransia and Xstriction!" The vine immediately unwound, flew through the air, and wrapped tightly around Bang's snout.

"There, your dog is muzzled," Volpe laughed. "He is now a canine with neither bark nor bite."

Raven flapped his wings and screeched, "You are a vile man and your arrogance is most unbecoming."

Volpe smiled and said, "You would lecture *me*? Your words are nothing but the squawking of a dirty fowl. Have you forgotten that Man was given dominion over all the lowly beasts of the field and birds of the air?" Volpe pointed again, repeated his incantation, and another vine wrapped suddenly around Raven, pinning his wings to his sides.

"Oh, how sad," Volpe said sarcastically. "What's worse than a bird who cannot take flight?"

Seeing his friend humiliated in such a manner, Nina Nita roared in anger, "You let him go! He's my friend. Let him go right now!"

Volpe pointed his finger and spoke, "Xvisio! Let him wander in the night; a pitiful bear with no sight." And Nina Nita was struck blind.

The bear lumbered about, roaring helplessly, swinging his great paws wildly in the air, hoping to strike his foe. But Volpe and his horse slipped easily away from the bear's grasp.

"Nina Nita, look out," Steven shouted. Too late. The bear stumbled over a rock and fell into the Black River.

Volpe laughed so hard he nearly fell off his horse. "Ah, you look thirsty, bear," Volpe mocked. "I think you should drink while you're in there. Yes, drink."

"No! Get out of the water," Steven said, trying to help Nina Nita out of the river. "Don't drink it. Remember what Alexia told us."

With darkness falling once again, Steven looked around at his friends as they floundered about helplessly. The three of them had rushed to Steven's defense with no thought for their own safety, and Volpe had quickly and easily struck them down. Steven was frantic, fearing what more Volpe might do to harm them.

"It's me you want," Steven said. "I'll come with you peacefully if you'll let them be."

Volpe rubbed his white goatee and considered. "You have caused me a great deal of aggravation, young Standing, but I am not without mercy. Ride with me and give me no trouble, and I will let your friends live."

"No, you've got to set them free and heal them. They wouldn't survive out here otherwise."

Amused by Steven's brashness, Volpe grinned at the boy. "You are indeed a feisty one, aren't you? Alright then, come with me, and they will return to normal and be released from their bonds by next light."

Steven studied the White Man for a long moment. Worried for his friends and seeing no other viable alternatives, he said, "Swear it. Give me your word."

Volpe nodded. "You have my word."

Steven kneeled next to Bang and Raven and put a hand gently on each. "I love you, my friends," he said. "But I have to go now."

Bang shook his head strongly from side to side in protestation. Raven spoke quietly, "You must not surrender to this evil man."

"Trust me," Steven whispered. "This isn't over."

"Enough with the goodbyes," Volpe said. "Now, climb on, young Standing. Let's get you back where you belong."

Steven slung his bag over his shoulder and leaped up behind Volpe on the horse's back. The great white stallion beat its wings and rose up into the night sky, carrying Steven Standing away from his friends and toward the luminous moon.

Chapter 12

Steven Standing held tight to Volpe's back as the winged horse flew high above the trees of the Ooljee Forest. He kept his eyes focused straight ahead, breathing slowly, and eschewing distractions – quite difficult, considering the circumstances – so that he might be able to formulate a plan of action. Soon Steven decided it best to engage Volpe in conversation, in hope that the White Man might unknowingly reveal something helpful.

"Are we heading back to the After City now?" Steven asked, shouting into the rushing wind.

"Of course," Volpe said.

"Why is it so important to you that I go back to the city?" Steven asked.

"Because The After is your new home according to the Will of Big Father. You must return for proper processing before your absence creates an even greater disturbance. Big Father would be most displeased by a 'missing person'.

"Who is Big Father?"

Volpe laughed loudly. "He is the ultimate authority and it would behoove you to get used to the idea quickly."

"None of this is fair, you know," Steven said. "I shouldn't be forced to live where I do not wish to be."

"Standing, there is no fair or unfair. There is only the Will of Big Father. The clay cannot resist the Potter."

"Can I meet Big Father?"

Again Volpe laughed, even louder than before. "Can a moth touch the Sun? Can an ant carry the moon? Can one grain of sand hold back the sea?"

Steven went silent for a moment and decided to abandon the topic. Instead, he asked, "How long will it take us to get back to the city?"

"Two shines of the moon."

"Will we stop along the way?"

"Stop wasting your breath with foolish questions," Volpe said. "You worry and talk excessively, young Standing. You are much like your ancestor."

"What do you mean? What ancestor?"

"Saveyon Standing. Many, many generations ago he stirred up trouble in The After, much like you. I knew your name sounded somehow familiar when I first met you on the day of your Hearing."

"What happened to him? What did he do?" Steven asked, his curiosity piqued.

"No more questions. You will soon be assimilated and acclimated into the Good Life of The After. Be at peace, my child."

Steven remembered the old man he'd seen on the day of his Hearing, in the Complaint Office of the Department of Human Relations Building. As Steven sat upon the white horse, the wind whistling in his ears, he recalled the look of the sorrow upon the man's face and the sadness in his voice. *I'm not going to end up like him, trapped in this crazy world*, Steven thought. *I've got to do something quickly, before we've gone much farther.*

Steven looked down. All he could see below was the topside of the forest, a thick, shrouded mass of dark foliage and shifting shadows dancing beneath the bulbous moon. He estimated that they were flying at least two hundred feet from the ground, though it was hard to tell for sure. He couldn't jump. What good would that do?

72

It was almost certain that he would not survive such a fall. And even if he did, Volpe would swoop down upon him quickly.

Steven tried to remember the counsel Alexia had given him, all the positive things she'd said about his calling and the power within him. *If her words were true,* Steven thought, *then things cannot end like this. There must be a way to escape.*

Steven felt the outline of The Ripper in the rucksack against his back. It seemed to be vibrating gently, sending out some sort of indescribable energy. Steven had an idea.

"I'd like a drink of water," Steven said. "I have some in my bag. Would you like a drink?"

"No," Volpe said sternly. "Drink your water and keep quiet."

Steven dug into his bag, pulled out a canteen, and casually took a drink. As he returned it back to the bag, he slipped the bat out slowly at the same time, careful that his actions would arouse no suspicions. Volpe was guiding the horse, watching the sky, paying little attention to Steven.

Steven clutched The Ripper close to his body, feeling it pulsate with energy, and wondered what to do next. He knew that Volpe's peripheral vision would allow him to easily see if he attempted to swing the bat at him as a weapon. But what else could he do? He remembered Alexia's words: *the bat has been kissed and empowered by the Eternal Fire.*

Steven looked down at the blur of forest passing beneath him, and up at the misty clouds that hung in the air like phantoms. He knew that with each passing second, he was growing closer to the bondage of The After.

In desperation, Steven thrust the meat end of The Ripper hard against Volpe's back. There was a flash of brilliant light and a surge of energy shot out of the bat and coursed through the White Man's body. He shuddered, screamed out in pain, and fell from the winged steed. For a moment, Volpe caught hold of the horse's mane and hung there. The horse bucked and twisted frantically in fear and confusion as Volpe dangled from its neck, his feet kicking wildly in the air as he tried to pull himself up.

Steven put the The Ripper to Volpe's chest and the power of the bat rippled once more through the White Man's body like an electrical charge. Stunned, Volpe lost his grip and plummeted into the darkness, screaming, "I will hunt you down and destroy you, Steven Standing! You will not escape me."

And then there was silence.

Steven had never ridden a horse before, certainly not one that could fly. He grasped the reins and tried to calm the frightened horse. "Easy, boy," he said softly, rubbing the neck of the beautiful equine. "It's okay now. Everything's okay."

In the struggle, the horse had circled wildly as it fought to stay aloft and Steven had become disoriented. He could no longer be sure in the darkness which direction they'd been traveling. "We want to go anywhere but the After City," he said softly to the horse. "Anywhere but there."

They held in place for a moment as Steven studied the moon. Finally, trusting his instincts, he guided the great, winged stallion in the direction that he hoped would take them deeper into the Ooljee Forest.

Chapter 13

Steven Standing directed the great beast to the ground after hours in the air, feeling a good bit proud of himself for having mastered the challenges of equestrian flight in a relatively short time. With an obvious swagger, he slid off the horse, lost his balance, and tumbled ingloriously onto his rear in the dirt. The horse looked back at Steven with a thoroughly puzzled expression.

Steven was first tempted to curse, but instead a grin spread slowly across his face. *I might as well laugh; this whole thing just keeps getting crazier and crazier.* And so he did. He laughed uncontrollably. He laughed until his sides hurt, while the horse simply ate some more grass.

"That's it? You have nothing to say? No smart-aleck remarks?" Steven said after he'd gotten control of himself. "You're just going to stand there eating grass?"

The horse raised his head and looked at Steven dumbly – ears twitching, tail swishing, teeth munching on a mouthful of long green strands – and said not a word.

"Oh, come on, now. Don't tell me you can't talk. Most of the other animals I've met in this messed-up place can talk. Now when I could really use some conversation, I end up with a horse that won't say a word."

The horse casually resumed chewing and Steven gave up. Standing, he tried to focus on his current predicament. "Okay, now what?" he said to himself. "I have no idea where I am, where my friends are, or where the Portal might be. And I saw no sign of the Black River, so I don't even know how to get back where I was before Volpe showed up."

The horse shook his head and made a snorting noise that vibrated its lips.

"And you're no help at all," Steven said.

Steven pulled his baseball from his bag and tossed it in the air as he paced back and forth. It helped him think more clearly, and he was hoping to come up with a plan.

Darkness came quickly and the huge, ever-present, full moon cast its eerie luminescence over the Ooljee Forest. The horse stomped and shifted nervously, and made uneasy whimpers deep in its throat as a cold wind blew across the land. Steven caught the horse's fear and felt himself trembling, though he could not tell why. Suddenly, a black mass crossed the sky, so thick that it nearly blotted out the monstrous moon. The darkness increased a hundred-fold and Steven could barely see his hand in front of his face.

There came a great rushing roar high above, like the beating of a million beastly wings. Something was happening, something that seemed to be of magnanimous portent, but Steven had no idea what it was. Overcome by terror, the horse panicked, ran across the clearing, and took off wildly into the sky.

"No! Stop! Come back!" Steven cried, but the horse paid him no mind.

When the black mass passed and the moonlight returned, Steven sat down beneath a tree and cried. He wanted to be strong, and he tried to be, but it was no use. *Why is this happening to me? Why won't this nightmare end? I just want to go home.*

Steven was hunched over, his head slumped forward, with The Ripper in his arms across his chest. He tried to focus on the things his dad had taught him about fighting through the tough times and never giving up. And he remembered Alexia's counsel, and tried to take comfort and find strength in her words. But it seemed like everything was just one big, jumbled mess in his mind. Tired and lonely, Steven muttered to himself, "I'm all alone out here...."

A voice whispered, "Yessss, that's right, poor boy. You are all alone."

"I don't even know where to go or what to do," Steven said.

"Yes, you're lost in this vast wilderness," the voice said.

"I've tried to be strong. I've done my best."

"But it wasn't good enough, was it?"

Lost in his misery, Steven shook his head *No*. His nose was running and his face was soaked with tears.

"You might as well give up," the voice suggested. "You've tried, but it's no use. You should just surrender."

Steven sniffed and sobbed softly.

"Give up. Put down the bat."

As if in a trance, Steven slowly began to lay The Ripper down at his side, but the bat pulsated and glowed brightly in his hand.

"Put the bat down," the voice demanded. "Put it down now."

Suddenly, somehow, the power of the Eternal Fire living in the bat surged through Steven Standing and brought him back to his senses. He opened his eyes and was shocked to see a snake staring at him, only inches away, hanging from a tree branch. The serpent had burning, beady eyes, rippling reptilian skin, and tiny dagger-like teeth. It smiled at him and hissed, "Well, then, I guess we'll have to do this the hard way."

The snake lunged forward, mouth open wide, pointy teeth shining, but Steven reacted quickly, instinctively, blocking the attack with The Ripper. He rolled and sprung to his feet in a flash, gripping the bat tightly as it burned with power and fury.

But the snake was not alone; it was the leader of an army of snakes, and they all dangled from the trees, hanging upside down, smiling the same wicked smile.

Steven gasped and stumbled backward for a moment when he saw how many there were. The snakes cackled like serpentine witches as they toyed with him, snapping at him almost playfully, as though they were smugly certain of victory.

And it made Steven angry, angrier than he'd ever been in his entire life. Trembling with rage, he bared fangs of his own, and hissed at the tree snakes, "It isn't over until the fat lady sings."

The lead snake, the one who'd first whispered in his ear, tilted his head to one side and furrowed his snaky brow, perplexed by Steven's odd remark. And then Steven smashed his skull with the bat.

The other snakes filled the forest with a horrible clamor of hellish hissing and screeching unlike anything Steven had ever heard. Some of the snakes recoiled and retreated back up into the trees, but a thousand others surged forward and attacked.

Steven roared into the battle and swung The Ripper in wild fury, ripping scores of serpents from the trees. As he waded through their midst, Steven felt several sharp tingles and prickles on his calves and back, but he ignored them and fought on. He was screaming with a soldier's rage in the heat of mortal combat. It was kill or be killed.

A hundred of his foes massed together and came at him as one huge ball of venom. Steven pointed The Ripper toward them and a blue-white streak of raw energy sizzled from the bat's end. It turned the slithering, slimy mass of reptiles into a smoking heap of burning, evil flesh. The stench was almost unbearable.

Steven felt more sharp stabs from behind and he suddenly realized he was being bitten. He'd been so consumed by the battle that he'd barely even felt the pain. Panic struck as he grasped the fact that venom must now be coursing through his body.

Surely that many bites will kill me, he thought. *How much time do I have left?* Steven spun in a circle, shooting powerful streams from the end of the bat. He had no idea how he was causing the energy to flow, but somehow, mysteriously, he was. Snakes were sizzling and shrieking in agony as the lightning bolts from The Ripper flashed in the night and tore through the forest.

And then it was over. Everything went silent and blurry as Steven Standing collapsed in the dirt beneath the leaves of a Succato Plant.

Chapter 14

Steven Standing, teetering on the brink of death, didn't feel the strong, knobby hands that lifted and carried him through the thick brush to a hidden tunnel. And he was completely unaware of being hauled down, down, down through a labyrinth of narrow stone passageways, winding ever more deeply below the surface.

The creatures who rescued the unconscious lad placed his swollen body on a soft bed of eider down and kendrith leaves, and tended to his wounds by the flickering light of kerosene torches. They rubbed a specially prepared mixture of warm clay, lobelia, fenugreek and other herbs into his skin before attaching leeches to his arms, legs and torso. On his tongue they placed seven drops of asimina triloba and eight drops of cayenne extract at regular intervals for two full days.

Steven slumbered in a deep sleep as his body slowly healed with the aid of the medicines he was given. His mind roamed far and wide in the land of dreams, and he saw himself standing in a field of golden wheat. The wind was blowing gently and the grain was moving beneath his hands, brushing softly against his fingertips in the sunlight. His mother and father were there, as were all his old friends, all laughing, happy, home.

At last, Steven's eyelids flickered open. Torch light and shadows danced together on the ceiling directly above him and on the rock walls around him, providing a luminosity that was slightly unnerving, yet warm and comforting at the same time. Nothing looked familiar and he couldn't remember what had happened to him. He lay perfectly still and listened. Wherever he was, it was a place filled with robust laughter and the happy chattering of spirited debate. He could hear voices but saw no one.

Suddenly, Steven became aware of a disgusting, almost unbearable taste in his mouth. His face contorted involuntarily and he gagged, "Yuuuuccckkk," turning the single word into a series of long, drawn out syllables.

A part-human creature rushed to Steven's side, and leaned in close with great concern. The face staring down at Steven was craggy, hairy, with a protruding brow and a fat nose. Steven gasped in surprise and horror.

The creature smiled and said, "You aren't exactly Sleeping Beauty yourself."

Another creature, similar to the first, appeared and placed a hand gently on Steven's shoulder. "My name is Dur. I am Dur of the Brisbanes," it said. "Don't be afraid. You're safe here with us. We found you in the Ooljee. You'd been bitten by many snakes--"

"Ah, yes, but you'd killed at least a thousand of them in the battle!" the first creature said. "Generally speaking, I believe in the 'Live and Let Live' philosophy, but there must be a line drawn somewhere, eh? I say we're all better off without those wicked reptiles. Well done, lad."

A third creature, whose name was Kiv, stepped into Steven's field of vision as he lay on the bed. Kiv was smaller than the other two, and wore glasses that kept sliding down his long, narrow nose. To Steven, he appeared to be the studious one of the three.

Taking issue with Bok's philosophical stance, Kiv said, "Bok, you're speaking out of both sides of your mouth. Just as you and I were discussing earlier today, complete autonomy – whether by the individual, by government, or by species – cannot be experienced within

81

the confines of an outsider's subjective parameters. You throw that expression around like it's--"

Dur interrupted them, tilting his head and motioning toward the young man on the bed of leaves. "Um, excuse me, brothers. Can we focus, please, on the matter at hand and save your discussion for a later time? We have more pressing matters to attend to."

"Yes, yes, of course," Bok said, slinging an arm around Kiv. "There will be plenty of time later to explain why I'm right and my comrade is most definitely wrong."

Seizing the opportunity to speak, Steven said, "Excuse me, sirs, but where am I exactly?"

"You are in the Under of The After," Dur answered. "We live far below the surface of the Ooljee Forest."

"You said I'd been bitten by many snakes..." Steven's voice trailed off as he tried hard to remember. "Yes, I do remember now. They were everywhere. They kept coming at me, more and more of them--"

"Yes, but you're safe now. Relax and rest," Dur said. "We have administered powerful medicines and the Droman Leeches are pulling the last of the toxins from your body. Give it a little more time."

"Leeches?" Steven raised his arms and gasped. "Uggh...get them off, get them off!" he shouted.

"Easy, easy now," Dur said. "You don't want to upset them."

"Upset *them*? What about *me*?"

"Lad, you wouldn't be alive right now if it weren't for those leeches. You should thank them."

Steven closed his eyes and tried to breathe deeply, to calm himself and to think positively as Alexia had taught him. Memories flooded in.

"My friends!" Steven said. "Volpe forced me to leave them behind. I've got to find them."

"Your friends?" Dur asked, raising one furry eyebrow. "Would that be a dog, a bear, and a raven?"

"Yes, that's them!" Steven said. "How did you know about them?"

"We have eyes in the Ooljee," Bok said.

"Where are they?" Steven asked excitedly.

"Last we heard, they were following the Black River through the valley," Dur said. "I do not do this lightly, young Mr. Standing, but for you, I will send out a pair of Brisbane trackers. I'll have your friends brought to the Great Hall in the Chasm of Caves so that you may be reunited with them."

"Is that really wise?" Kiv asked softly. "What of our secrecy? Perhaps we should bring this matter before the Council."

"There is no time for that," Dur said. "It is a calculated risk; one I feel we must take under the circumstances."

"Sleep now," Dur said, turning back to Steven. "The healing process is still underway within you. Once you are up and around, we will give you some proper Under food and answer all your questions."

Chapter 15

Steven Standing was so hungry when he awoke on the third day that he didn't mind that the food on his plate was moss stew and lichen bread. It smelled delicious, and as for the taste, Steven ate so quickly that he was hardly aware of it.

"Whoa, slow down, boy," Bok said, his own mouth full of stew.

Steven had barely noticed the crowd of Brisbanes seated around him in the large dining hall. They were also eating while watching him with earnest curiosity, anxious to hear his story.

The Brisbanes were a short people, less than five feet tall, and they walked in a hunched-over position which further added to their height-challenged appearance. They were also quite hairy with broad shoulders and large feet and hands; and they wore nothing but loincloths, unless, of course, you count eyeglasses.

When Steven finished his meal, he leaned back and rubbed his stomach. "That was delicious. I apologize for eating so fast and finishing before the rest of you," he said. "I was just so hungry and hadn't had an actual hot meal in a long time."

"It is a good sign to see you with a hearty appetite," Dur said. "You are a fast healer."

"I do want to thank you...for everything," Steven said. "I suppose I'd be dead right now if it weren't for all of you."

Bok slapped him genially on the back. "Think nothing of it. You'd have done the same for any one of us. I can see it in your eyes."

Dur stood at the head of the long table, cleared his throat, and all the Brisbanes gave him their attention, even those who were still eating.

"As you have no doubt heard, we have an impressive, young human with us today. He is Steven Standing, the snake-killer," Dur began. Several of the Brisbanes raised their mugs and voiced their agreement, shouting *Indeed!* and *Aye!*

"All of you probably have questions you'd like to ask him," Dur continued, smiling at Steven, "And I'm quite sure, if he's feeling up to it, he will do his best to give you answers."

Steven was rather embarrassed by all the attention, but he replied, "Yes, of course. I'll be glad to answer your questions...if I can."

"But first, I think it wise that young Mr. Standing learn a little more about us," Dur said. The old Brisbane straightened his dark green, ceremonial robe, clasped his hands together, and cleared his throat loudly.

"The Brisbanes are an ancient tribe who came here to the Under from The Before," Dur began. "Nearly a quarter of a million years ago, we were an off-shoot of the group humans call *homo neanderthalensis*, although we were, and still are, far more intelligent and advanced than our descendants have ever given us credit for--"

Interrupting, Bok slapped his hairy hands on his knobby knees and roared with laughter, "Ah, yes, I've heard that in their textbooks, arrogant *Homo sapiens* show us pushing a crude stone wheel around or running from fire like dim-witted chimpanzees!"

"But it was truly quite the contrary, young Standing," Dur said. "In those days, we were developing genetic codes, charting the stars, and building a better mousetrap. At least, until the Great Catastrophe."

"The Great Catastrophe?" Steven asked.

"We think it was a meteor," Kiv interjected. "Although it's difficult to ascertain for certain from our present position in the Under of The After."

"Besides, that was a very, very long time ago," Bok said, stuffing a curried fritter in his mouth. "We stopped trying to figure it out."

"Not all of us," Kiv said. "Some of us never weary of learning."

Dur cleared his throat and continued, "Let's not digress. Suffice to say, none of our primate relatives were as technologically or intellectually advanced as we. Most of them fell somewhere between the Mousterean and Acheulean Tool Periods on the evolutionary ladder."

Steven raised his hand. "If I may ask a question...are you saying that you are ancestors of humans? Like the missing link or something?"

"Ancestors, yes. Missing link, well that's something else entirely. Unfortunately, however, our civilization as we knew it then, was destroyed by the Great Catastrophe. We have been here in the Under of The After ever since. We dug out these caves ourselves over the millennia, always staying hidden, especially from those in the After City and from the eyes of Big Father."

"Debatable," Kiv said, pushing his glasses up on his long, narrow nose. "If Big Father is all that the legends say He is, then how can anyone truly hide from his sight, eh?"

"This is neither the time nor place to argue that subject," Dur said. Then, to Steven he said, "As you have probably surmised, we are an intellectual and gregarious people who revel in spirited conversation, inquisitive investigation, and healthy debate."

"Yes, I have noticed that," Steven said. "Why do you keep hidden down here? Is it because, like me, you escaped from the After City?"

"No, we were never assigned to the City, but rather to the Ooljee Forest," Kiv said. "Don't get me started on the systematic and on-going discriminatory process that seems so ingrained--"

"Great boar bristles!" Bok laughed. "Indeed, please don't get him started." Several of the other Brisbanes chuckled.

"Wait," Dur interrupted. "Steven, did you say you escaped from the After City?"

"Yes, I ran into the forest with my dog, Bang. It was there that I met Raven, Nina Nita and Alexia. All I'm trying to do is get back home, back to The Before--"

"You met Alexia, the great She-Wolf?" Dur asked incredulously.

"Yes. She helped me get started on my journey to the Portal. And she saved me and my friends from a pack of wild wolves," Steven replied. "I don't know what happened to her after that." Steven hung his head sadly and rubbed his temples, which were now starting to pound again.

"Are you okay, young Standing?" Bok asked.

"It's just that so much has happened so quickly," Steven said. "I guess I'm just feeling a bit overwhelmed. I still can't shake the feeling that all of this is just a very bad dream."

"Perhaps we should let Steven return to bed," Dur suggested. "It may be we are taxing him too much with our questions, so soon after his injuries."

"No, no," Steven said. "I'll be fine. I've had more than enough of being in bed."

"So, how did you come to be in a battle with those vile reptiles?" Bok asked. "And more importantly, how did you kill so many of them? The only weapon we found was a wooden club. Is that what you used?"

"It's a complicated story," Steven said. "But, yes, that club is my weapon. It's a baseball bat that I call The Ripper."

"Must be quite an impressive weapon with some sort of hidden power," Bok said.

"Yes, Alexia had me put it in something she called the Eternal Fire. I don't understand what she did to it, but it worked. I also used it to defeat Volpe. Have you heard of him?"

The room became very quiet.

"Volpe, the White Man?" Dur asked. "You defeated the White Man?"

"Well, yes, I suppose so...actually, I just sort of knocked him off his horse," Steven said somewhat sheepishly.

The Brisbanes were speechless as they took in Steven's words. Some stopped chewing in mid-bite. Some choked on their drinks. Bok's mouth hung open and lichen biscuit fell out. But after a moment of stunned silence, they began to cheer and shout Steven's name.

Dur quieted the crowd, then turned to Steven. "So, young Standing, I must ask – what did the White Man do when you knocked him off his horse?"

Steven, wishing he had a better answer, bit the inside of his jaw as he looked around the room at the expectant faces of the Brisbanes. "Well, I...I don't know...he just...fell."

The room erupted with laughter, and again Dur quieted his brethren. "But Steven, did he not become angry or fight back?"

"He couldn't," Steven said. "We were two hundred feet in the air. So, like I said, he just fell."

Immediately, there was a joyous uproar in the dining room, an enthusiastic eruption of laughter, celebratory cheers and shouts greater than any Steven had ever heard at any ballgame or concert. Some of the Brisbanes pounded their mugs on the tables while others danced around the room with delight.

"I take it that Volpe's not very popular here," Steven said with a smile, his first one in a while.

Bok laughed loudly and tousled Steven's golden locks with a big, hairy hand. "Aye, young Standing! The White Man is about as well liked as a beetle fungus on one's backside!"

Chapter 16

Steven Standing was exhausted by the time the Brisbanes finished hugging and congratulating him. As Dur, Bok and Kiv walked him back to his room, Steven could still hear many of the others singing his praises in the Great Hall.

"I feel pretty embarrassed by all this," Steven said, stooping as he walked beneath the low ceilings of the Under. "I mean, I appreciate it...don't get me wrong. You're all most kind. But I don't think I did anything special; I just did what I had to do."

"Ah, yes," Bok said, putting a muscled, hairy arm around Steven. "That's what heroes always say. You are ever the modest one, young Standing."

"You know, it's been a very long time since we've heard such exciting and good news from the surface," Kiv said.

"And even longer since we've had a visitor from above," Dur added. "Rarely in our history have we allowed outsiders to come here. Our privacy and secrecy is of the utmost importance. Our survival as a society may very well depend upon it."

"That's right," Bok said. "We rarely go to the surface and actually set foot in The After."

"Then how did you even know about me? And what made you decide to rescue me and bring me here to your home? Why did you risk it?" Steven asked.

"As for how we knew about you, we have several reconnaissance methods," Kiv said. "We have a select few sentries who keep ears and eyes on the Ooljee Forest. We also maintain a complex series of vision holes, sensors and sight tunnels. And we keep in contact with a very select few of the animals on the surface."

"As for why we risked our secrecy to rescue you," Dur said. "That is a thing of the spirit, Steven, and hard to explain. Great forces seem to be coming together in recent times, and there has long been a prophecy, scoffed at by many, of the Mistake who would become the Savior. Some have said it would be a young human male, and I happen to believe that."

"I've heard that expression before about the Mistake and Savior," Steven said.

"How did you hear of the prophecy?" Kiv asked.

"First from someone in the City, then from Alexia herself," Steven answered. "But I don't understand it, and I don't know what it has to do with me. Like I've told everyone all along – I'm just a kid trying to get home to my parents and friends, to get back to my life."

"Back to your life?" Kiv said. "Isn't *this* your life right here and now?"

"You know what the boy means," Bok interjected. "Don't trouble his brain with your philosophical complexities."

"Yes, but crisis points are the greatest teaching opportunities of all, are they not?" Kiv persisted. "Here Steven is faced with great challenges, and I say this is precisely the time for him to consider these important issues."

"But as I was saying," Dur continued. "Strange forces are at work, Steven. Just a short time before we found you unconscious in the Ooljee, we heard of a mysterious mass of darkness or winged evil – we're not sure what it was – moving across the sky, nearly blocking out the moon"

"Yes, I remember! I saw that," Steven said. "It came right before the snakes attacked, and it's what scared away my-- I mean, Volpe's horse. I wonder what it could have been."

"We don't know," Dur said as they reached Steven's room.

"But we're pretty sure it's not good," Bok added. "Not good at all."

"There are urgent matters that require my attention, so I must take my leave for the evening," Dur said. "Steven, you should get some rest."

"Rest? I'm tired but I'm too excited to sleep," Steven said. "And I have so many questions."

"Perhaps Bok and Kiv will sit with you and answer your inquiries," Dur said. "Good night, Steven."

"Good night, Mr. Dur," Steven said as the short, hairy fellow lumbered down the dark hallway and out of sight.

"So, young Steven," Bok said, "What questions do you have for us?"

"I'm not sure where to begin," Steven said, sitting down on his bed of leaves. "What can you tell me about Volpe? Who or what is he, exactly?"

"He is one of the leading Ministers in Big Father's Kingdom," Kiv said. "It is a position of great power--"

"And you know what they say about power," Bok interjected. "It corrupts."

"And his is a corruption of the most despicable brand," Kiv continued. "He represents the Holy of Holies, yet, whether he fully realizes it or not, he does the works of the Great Serpent. It is a hypocrisy most vile; a man in white whose heart abides in darkness, and who justifies his cruelty by conducting it beneath the banner of Big Father."

"And just who is this Big Father I keep hearing about?" Steven asked.

"He's the ultimate authority," Bok said.

"You mean, like God?" Steven said.

"Ah, yes, he does *so* want to be thought of in that manner," Kiv said. "But Big Father could be more accurately described as a sort of authoritative, egotistical, political manifestation of the God-like persona."

"Oh, boar bristles!" Bok said. "Big Father is God."

"Come now, Bok. You are a Brisbane of reasonable intelligence, yet you persist in holding positions that are contradictory one to the other. If Big Father is truly the God you think he is, how can he not know, as you have often purported, of our existence here in the Under? If he is a god at all, then he must be a lesser god, like those of some ancient mythology such as the Greek or Norse. So which is it, Bok? Is he omniscient or is his knowledge limited?"

"It's not a simple matter of either-or, as you are trying to make it out to be," Bok replied. "Big Father chooses to have *selective* knowledge. He knows we're down here below the surface, but He chooses to look the other way for now, and the reasons are His alone."

"Oh, how utterly ridiculous," Kiv said. "Your argument is akin to the ancient question *Can God make a rock so big that He can't lift it?*"

Steven interrupted their discussion. "Tell me, if Big Father – whoever or whatever he is – is in charge of things, then is he the one who brought me here to The After?"

Simultaneously, Kiv answered *No* and Bok *Yes*.

"That's a big help," Steven said with a smile. He picked up The Ripper and rolled it easily between his hands, then stood and took a few smooth practice swings. "I miss baseball," he said, changing the subject.

"How does that thing work?" Bok asked. "I mean, how do you unleash its power for snake-killing and the like."

Steven shrugged. "Truth is, I don't really know. When I'm in a tough spot, fighting for my life, it just seems to happen somehow."

"I believe I can answer that," Kiv explained. "The She-Wolf must have used the Eternal Fire to infuse the club with cosmic powers and to establish a direct molecular link between you and the weapon."

"That's what I thought," Bok laughed.

"Well, that kind of power will sure come in handy when I'm facing a 98 mph fastball from a major league pitcher."

Steven took up a batter's stance in the center of the room and tapped the bat on his insoles. Crouching low, he wiggled the bat overhead and concentrated on a make-believe pitcher's mound in his mind's eye. Bok and Kiv watched the odd behavior with puzzled expressions.

Steven swung at the imaginary pitch with all his might and shouted, "Back, back, back...Can 'a corn! It's out'ta here!"

Bok scratched his furry head and said, "Can of corn? You are a most unusual boy, Steven Standing."

Chapter 17

Steven Standing felt the tremor as he sat in his room, staring at his lifeless phone, wishing he could pull up the pictures it contained. Then the rumble rolled over him like the sound of a dozen hell-trains hauling a heavy load of misery. Dust and small stones filtered down from the ceiling, torches shook in their holders, and Brisbane artwork fell from the walls of his bedroom.

Steven grabbed The Ripper and rushed out into the dim hallway where dozens of the Brisbanes were running to and fro. "What's happening?" Steven shouted.

"Could be an earthquake," one of them said.

"Sounds like a battle of some sort," another said.

Steven grabbed his backpack and ran through the maze of narrow corridors to the Great Assembly Room. Dur, Bok and Kiv were already there, attempting to calm and organize their people.

"Quiet, my brothers, quiet," Dur was saying, waving his arms in the air. "Listen to me. Do not panic."

There were shouts from the crowd: *What's happening? Are we in danger? Are we under attack?*

One of the tallest Brisbanes stepped to the front and said, "It's because of the human boy!"

"Maybe they're coming for him!" another shouted.

Confusion and unrest were spreading quickly, and though most of the Brisbanes supported Steven, some had been, from the very beginning, less enthusiastic about his ongoing presence in their midst, fearing it would endanger the secrecy and safety of their way of life.

Dur put his hand on the shoulder of the tall Brisbane in a congenial manner, hoping to defuse the tension. "I remind you that we don't yet know the nature of the disturbance above. It may merely be a natural phenomenon of some type, a large storm or an earthquake, for example."

"All this time we've been here, I've never heard anything that sounded quite like this," a very old Brisbane said, puffing on a cob pipe. "Might be we should move to the Fortress Chamber, just to be safe."

"Yes, yes, an excellent and most prudent suggestion," Dur conceded. "Let's gather our necessities and move there in an orderly manner. That will give us time to hear from our sentries, ascertain the potential danger, and develop a course of action."

As the crowd dispersed, Dur shook his head with great disappointment and said, "Steven, I apologize that you had to hear those unsavory comments from some of the brethren."

"It's that troublesome Grotte clan," Bok said. "Pay them no heed, young Steven. They're always finding fault, running scared, or putting themselves in a snit about something."

"But what if they're right?" Steven asked. "What if Volpe survived the fall and he's come searching for me with some sort of army? I'd hate to be the cause of trouble for your people."

Another Brisbane, one Steven had not seen before, swaggered toward them. He was hairy like the others, but with a gray beard so long that it nearly reached the ground. "Heard what you said about us, Bok," he muttered.

"Heard it, but can't deny the truth of it, can you?" Bok retorted.

"This is Lindle, chief of the Grotte clan," Dur said as introduction. Steven reached out hesitantly to shake Lindle's hand, but the Brisbane ignored him and said, "No one, human or otherwise, can resist Big Father or embarrass the White Man, as this human has, and expect to go unpunished. His sins will find him out."

"Since when did you care so much about what Volpe or Big Father thinks or does?" Bok asked.

"My concern is for the safety of our people and the security of our homeland here in the Under," Lindle said. "Would that your priorities were as straight as mine."

"In my opinion, Steven Standing may be vitally important to our survival," Dur said.

"Foolishness!" Lindle snorted, looking at Steven with disdain. "You have been deceived by this human boy who arrogantly thinks he can overcome the Great Serpent and somehow pass through the Portal."

"Sir, I'm just trying to get home," Steven said. "I don't mean to cause problems for you. Your people saved me in the Ooljee and I really--"

"We should have left you be," Lindle interrupted. "Now look what has come upon us."

As the Brisbanes argued, Steven found an opportunity to slip away inconspicuously and blend into the general commotion. With his pack on his back, he headed in the general direction of the Chasm of Caves, as it had been pointed out to him earlier, where he assumed he would find the exit leading to the Great Gulf, and eventually the Portal.

"Excuse me," Steven said, stopping a young Brisbane. "Is it far to the Great Hall?"

"A long day's journey, I think," the Brisbane said. "At least that's what I've heard. I've never been."

"Do you know if the way is marked somehow? Are there signs?"

"I only know that they say to follow the middle cave."

"Thank you," Steven said and rushed down the dark hallway alone.

Chapter 18

Steven Standing plunged into the unknown. At first there were torches hung at regular intervals that cast eerie light and dancing shadows upon the cave walls; but soon the torches grew farther apart until, eventually, darkness ruled. Steven pulled The Ripper from his bag and willed the bat to glow and give off its soft illumination.

The passageway was narrow with very low ceilings, more suitable for the short Brisbanes than a human teenager who was nearly six feet tall. And as Steven pressed deeper into the Chasm of Caves, the corridor grew ever smaller until eventually he was forced to proceed on hands and knees. Even with the light from his weapon, the darkness was oppressive, and the walls seemed to be crushing in upon Steven. His breath grew labored and great drops of sweat ran down his face and dripped from his chin. A claustrophobic wave of fear swept over the young man and threatened to drown him in panic and disillusionment. Steven's thoughts ran wild: *What if I followed the wrong cave? What if I never find the way out? I can't get enough breath! I'm going to die in here.*

In desperation, Steven stopped, closed his eyes, and clutched The Ripper tightly to his chest. He pictured his mother's smiling face, auburn hair, and the look of love shining in her brown eyes for her only remaining son. And he remembered how much fun he and his father had shooting hoops together in the driveway, and working on science projects in their small, basement lab. He loved his parents so very much, and his eyes filled with tears as he reminisced.

Then Steven let his thoughts drift to the ball field where his teammates would be taking infield practice and shagging flies. He could hear the crack of the bat and the cheers of the people in the bleachers. His girlfriend, Emily, was leaning against the chain link fence, watching the game, waving at Steven. He could see her cute dimples, jade eyes, and dark hair dancing on the breeze. Steven smiled as the pleasant memories washed over him, and renewed his spirit and resolve. *I can do this*, he told himself. *I know I can.*

Steven pressed on through the ever-shrinking passageway until finally it was no more than a foot high, and he was forced to crawl through seams and crevasses on his belly. The rocks below and above were sharp and jagged, and they cut into his back, stomach and thighs as he squeezed through. The only sounds were Steven's labored breathing and the scrape of his body over rock and dirt. At times the openings in the rock were so small that Steven could only get through by exhaling fully and sucking in his stomach as far as possible. If he took a breath, his chest would expand and he would be wedged there momentarily, caught literally between a rock and a hard place. The entire process was further complicated by his backpack. Steven was forced to take it off his back, flatten and smooth it as much as possible, and drag it behind him by tethering it to his ankle.

The passageway turned steeply downward and widened a bit, and the stone became slick with a film of running water. Steven began sliding headfirst on his belly down the narrow channel, and could only slow his descent by bracing his hands, elbows and feet hard against the walls. But as the grade grew sharper, he could no longer hold himself back, and soon was sliding faster and faster over the rough rocks. Steven banged against the walls, bouncing from side to side like a ball in a pinball machine; and somewhere along the way, he lost his grip on The Ripper.

The corridor widened abruptly and Steven was suddenly in free-fall, tumbling in blackness, his own yell of surprise echoing endlessly around him. He hit the floor hard, his left shoulder – the same one that had been injured by the wolves – taking the brunt of the impact. His backpack, having torn loose from his ankle, crashed in a heap across Steven's legs, while The Ripper landed somewhere in the darkness of the cavern.

Aside from the ringing in Steven's ears, the room was quiet for what seemed like a very long time, though it may have been only a moment. As the ringing subsided, Steven heard the slow but steady drip of water plopping into a shallow basin somewhere nearby. Bleeding, battered and sore, he lay on his back, unmoving, just on the edge of consciousness in the dirt, and counted five seconds between the drops. There was something peaceful, almost comforting in the gentle sound. Plop. Plop. Plop.

Soon another noise manifested itself, a ruffling, shuffling sort of sound, as though something was moving toward Steven very slowly in the blackness. He could hear it breathing, ever so faintly, as it came closer, closer.

Steven remained as still as possible, attempting to control his fear. His eyes were wide open, big as saucers, trying to see something, anything in the utter darkness, but there wasn't even a speck of light. The Ripper had ceased its illuminating glow, with the connection between boy and bat having been temporarily severed by the fall.

Steven heard a sound like the scraping of metal against rock, and then everything went silent. He held his breath until he was about to burst, straining to hear the shuffling noise or the breathing, but there was nothing.

Finally, a strained, high-pitched voice whispered, "Have you come to rescue me? Because if you have, you're not doing a very good job of it."

Chapter 19

Steven Standing stammered, "Um, well, do you *need* to be rescued?"

"Of course I need to be rescued," the squeaky voice in the darkness said. "Do you think I enjoy being chained up in this horrible place?"

"I'm sorry, I didn't know. Yes, I'll rescue you."

"Never mind," the voice said. "Your chivalry is dead if I have to beg for it."

"Please let me help you," Steven said. "And we'll get out of here together."

"Okay, then, you can rescue me. By the way, my name is Emma, Emma Free. Aren't you going to shake my hand?"

"I can't see your hand," Steven said. "Where are you?"

"Oh, that's right. You just got here. I've been here a very, very long time. My eyes have adjusted over the ages so that I can see just a tiny bit, vague shapes and shadows mostly. It's true what they say about your other senses, you know. They do become heightened. I can hear a worm eating a morsel, and I can smell a hyacinth blooming on the surface, even all the way down here. You don't believe me, do you?"

Steven's head was reeling, not only from the fall, but from Emma's rambling diatribe. She spoke more quickly than anyone Steven had ever heard, and her voice was similar to the chirping of a bird. Before he could respond to any of her questions or comments, she had already proceeded on to her next topic.

"Well, I suppose it really doesn't matter whether you believe me or not," Emma said. Steven felt a small hand take his and shake it vigorously. "You have come to rescue me and I am grateful. It is a pleasure to meet you. Aren't you going to tell me your name?"

"I'm Steven Standing, and it's good to meet you too. I was starting to wonder if..."

"You're not disappointed, are you? Say, did you come here from The After? Do you think I'm pretty?"

"No, no, I mean, yes," Steven was stammering again. "What I mean is...well, I can't even see you, so how can I know if you're pretty? But I'm sure you must be."

"The Great Serpent put me here because he said I was ugly. In fact, he said I was the ugliest girl in all of creation."

"Well, I'm sure that's not true," Steven said, quite uncomfortable with the conversation in general and this topic in particular.

"How do you know it's not true?" Emma asked. "Have you seen all the girls in creation?"

Steven rolled his eyes and hoped that the strange girl in the cave did not see.

There was a long awkward silence and then Steven heard a sniffling sound in the darkness. "Are you...are you crying?" Steven asked.

"No, I am not crying," Emma said defiantly. "Okay, yes, I am crying."

"But why?"

"You came here to rescue me and I've been nothing but rude to you. I apologize. I would not blame you one bit if you went on without me and left me here to rot. But you shouldn't. Do you know why you shouldn't?"

Steven hesitated.

"Because you need me," Emma continued.

"I do?"

"You are looking for the Portal, aren't you? I bet you are. Am I right?"

Surprised, Steven answered, "Yes, yes, I am. How did you--"

"Well, I know exactly where it is," Emma said. "All you have to do is set me free of this chain."

"Chain?"

"I told you I was chained here by the Great Serpent," Emma said curtly. "Here, give me your hand. Feel the chain?"

"Yes, I feel it," Steven answered.

"I have tried everything over the years. I tried scraping it on the sharp edge of the wall. I tried pounding on it with rocks. I even tried digging around the base where it's attached, hoping to pull the whole thing up and carry it with me. But nothing worked. The chain is fortified by the evil of the Great Serpent, and as long as I am imprisoned by it, my own powers are suppressed."

Steven ran his hands along the chain, and stopped suddenly. "Is it attached...around your neck?"

"Yes. Had it been around my ankle or wrist, I would have gnawed off my foot or hand long ago in order to get free. But the Serpent was too clever for that. He knew I couldn't very well lop off my own head."

"Yes, you wouldn't get far without that," Steven said with a bit of a laugh.

"I bet you are much stronger than I," Emma said. "You can probably snap the chain in two with your bare hands."

"Well...sure...I can probably do that...maybe," Steven said. But the chain was massive, as though it had been forged in the fires of hell; and Steven strained and pulled and twisted with all his might, but to no avail.

"My hero," Emma said dryly.

"I'm doing the best I can," Steven said, becoming irritated.

"I heard some things fall with you. Maybe you have a tool or weapon of some type that you could use to cut the chain."

Steven had been so distracted by the strange girl in the cave that he'd briefly forgotten about his backpack and bat. "Yes, you're right. Maybe I do have something that will help set you free."

Steven crawled about on his hands and knees in the darkness, feeling carefully for The Ripper. "Ah, here it is," he said, and the bat began to glow in his hand, giving off its soft white light.

Steven turned back toward the girl and gasped with surprise. Even though she'd apparently been chained in this tomb-like cavern for a very long time, Emma was absolutely beautiful, perfect even, as though it was magically so even in the midst of her dire predicament.

"What is it? What's wrong?" Emma asked. "Am I hideous as the Serpent said?"

Steven held The Ripper up and studied the young girl. Her blonde hair flowed about her in long strands and wisps, and her eyes were like the sky on a sunny day. She had a cute, little nose and pink lips that bore the most adorable, pouty expression.

"Hideous? Certainly not," Steven said. "I think the Great Serpent must be a *very* poor judge of beauty."

Chapter 20

Steven Standing placed the tip of The Ripper very carefully against the thick, metal band around Emma's neck. "Hold very still," Steven said as he closed his eyes and concentrated. The bat grew brighter and hotter as it surged with energy, and the chain began to glow red with heat.

"Stop, stop! It's too hot!" Emma screamed and pulled away.

"I'm so sorry," Steven said. "Are you okay?"

"I'll be alright in a minute," she said, rubbing her neck.

"I was trying to weaken the band itself so we could get it off your neck," Steven explained. "But I guess I'll have to break one of the links, and you'll have to carry the rest of the chain with you."

"I don't mind as long as I can be free of this prison and regain my powers."

Steven placed the fat end of the Louisville Slugger inside one of the large chain links. "Cover your eyes. I'm still learning how to control the power of this thing." he said, as he concentrated once again on channeling his wishes through the bat. The Ripper vibrated and hummed as hot, bluish-white energy flowed slowly into the chain link. Bit by bit, the metal glowed ever brighter, softened and stretched until it cracked open.

"You did it!" Emma shouted. "I'm free at last! Thank you." She hugged Steven and kissed him on the cheek, and his face flushed as red as the chain had been moments before.

Emma leaped to her feet with the remainder of the chain still dangling from her neck and hanging down past her waist. "I hope I still have my powers," she said.

"What are these powers you keep mentioning?" Steven asked.

"I have the Yellow Power. My Grammy gave it to me long ago. But as long as the Serpent's chain binds me, it cancels out my powers."

"What in the world does Yellow Power mean?"

"It is far too complicated and would require a long conversation. Yellow Power involves primary colors, square roots, the Four Winds and certain selective variations. It will be much easier if I simply demonstrate," Emma said. She took a deep breath, pointed at the stone wall before them, and spoke a verse:

> "*Lamb chops and mutton balls;*
> *I am weary of these walls.*
> *For too long I have been jailed;*
> *Open up the doors now veiled.*"

Bright yellow sparks danced from her fingertips and tickled the wall. Slowly the stone faded away and a long corridor appeared before them.

"Yes!" Emma said, dancing and twirling with joy. "After all this time, I still have it."

"Wow," Steven said. "Seriously, how did you do that?"

"Ladies never tell their secrets," Emma giggled and then plopped straight down on the dirt floor of the cavern.

"What are you doing?" Steven asked. "Are you okay?"

"I will be. When I use my powers, it makes me weak for a little while," she explained. "That was merely a tiny spell, but since it's been so long since the last time I cast one, I guess I got rather dizzy." Emma crossed her legs Indian-style and sat with her spine straight, head high, and eyes closed in deep meditation. Steven shuffled uncomfortably and tried not to stare at Emma, but it was hard for him to take his eyes off her.

Five minutes later, she jumped up and said, "Now get your things. We must go!" She grabbed Steven's hand and pulled him down the stone hallway.

As they ran, Steven asked, "Did you create this passageway or was it here all along, hidden from our eyes?"

"Exactly!" Emma shouted.

"I have a lot of questions for you," Steven said. "I sure hope you have some better answers than that."

"You can find out just as soon as we get out of here. I can bear no more of this place!"

They raced together down the long tunnel toward a pinprick of white far in the distance, stopping every so often to allow Emma to rest. As they got closer and closer to the mouth of the cave, the light grew brighter and Steven smelled fresh air and mysterious flora and fauna.

Finally, they burst out into the open and Steven nearly went soaring into space.

"Look out!" Emma shouted, grabbing Steven by arm and jerking him backwards. "We are on the edge of a cliff."

"Whoa! I see that now," Steven shouted as he scrambled to safety and got his balance.

"Sorry, I should have warned you but I was so excited about being free."

"That's okay," Steven said, standing on the short, narrow ledge, looking out across miles of thick, foreboding jungle that stretched to the far horizon.

"That is the Geni Jungle," Emma said, locking her arm in Steven's. "It is the domain of the Great Serpent and a terrifying place. That's where he captured me before imprisoning me in that cave where I've been for so very long." She shivered and Steven nervously put an arm around her. They stood that way for a short while, enjoying the grand vista before them, happy to be free from the oppressive blackness of the Chasm of Caves.

Finally, Steven said, "And after the jungle we'll find the Portal?

"No. Beyond the Geni are the Mirror Land and the Zero Line. If we make it that far, there we will find the Portal."

"We'll make it," Steven said.

Emma searched Steven's eyes with hers. "I hope so."

"Do we have to go through the jungle?" Steven asked. "Could we take another route?"

"There is no other way. To get to the Portal we must cross it, and pray that the Backwards Lookers will then grant us access to the Portal."

"And back to The Before," Steven said.

"Yes, I have heard that it is possible," Emma said. "But first, I must use a small spell to remove this chain from my neck." She placed her dainty hands on the metal band, closed her eyes, and spoke:

> *"Maple syrup and pancakes high,*
> *Roasted duck on toasted rye,*
> *Butter up and squiggle down,*
> *Loose this chain with which I'm bound."*

Bits of soft yellow light flowed gently from Emma's fingers and the band around her neck slowly widened, eventually doubling its circumference. Then, with a girlish grin, she slipped it over her head, and tossed it aside. "No more chain," she said. "Now let's rest here until night. Then we will venture down to the jungle under cover of darkness."

"Sounds good to me," Steven said. "But just listening to your spell made me even hungrier than I already was. Two days spent climbing through caves really works up an appetite."

"There are some grubs there between those rocks," Emma suggested.

"Yum," Steven said. "Grubs."

"They will sustain you for a while."

"It's weird," Steven began. "When I first got to this crazy place, it seemed as though I barely needed food, drink or sleep. But lately, I've been feeling much more hungry and sleepy with every passing day."

"That is because you have been traveling steadily away from the After City. And the further away from it you go, the closer you get to the Portal and The Before Restrictions. Thus, the Life Laws of The After have less and less effect on you."

Steven bit his lip and stared at Emma. "Right. Makes perfect sense," he said with a wry grin.

Chapter 21

Steven Standing sat on the ground, rolling The Ripper absently in his hands, and watching Emma Free as she dozed off and on. He had so much he wanted to talk to her about, so many things he was anxious to ask her, but didn't want to disturb her. He tried to think about something else. He pictured Raven and Nina Nita and it made him smile; and he missed Bang terribly. *I hope they're somewhere safe until I can get back to them.* He let his mind wander and his thoughts drifted back to home, his parents and friends, his old life.

Steven dug through his backpack and pulled out his cell phone. It was dead – he knew that – but he just wanted to check it again to be sure. He stared at it sadly.

"You are thinking about your parents," Emma said, startling Steven. "I recognize that look."

"Yes."

"Do you have any pictures of them?" Emma asked. "Maybe in that bag you carry? I'd like to see them, if you do."

"Well, I did have pictures. But they're on here," Steven said, holding up his phone. "And the battery's dead so I can't access them."

"Perhaps you could power it up with your bat," Emma suggested.

"I thought of that but I'd be afraid to try it," Steven said. "I'd probably fry the phone. It would be like trying to light a cigarette with a flame thrower."

"So, then, tell me about them," Emma said.

"Who?"

"Your parents, silly. What are they like?"

Steven thought for a moment and said, "My mom is the best. She's one of those moms that's always there, worrying about me, looking out for me, ya know?"

Emma smiled and nodded.

"I mean, sometimes I guess she can be a little embarrassing, but I know it's just because she loves me."

"And your father?"

"We do everything together. When I was three years old, he had me out in the yard, tossing a baseball back and forth. He bought me my first chemistry set and taught me everything. He's a scientist; did I tell you that?"

Emma shook her head no.

"Yeah, he does biochemical research at the Los Alamos Lab, top secret stuff. He's won a lot of awards for his work. I really don't think there's anything he can't do or figure out."

"It sounds as though you were blessed to be part of a wonderful family," Emma said.

"A lot of my friends don't get along with their parents at all. It's almost like they hate each other," Steven said. "I guess I'm an oddball, but it was never like that for me. I was always pretty close to my folks, especially after my brother..."

Steven fell silent as tears welled up in his eyes.

"Your brother?" Emma asked.

"I don't want to talk about that."

Emma reached out and stroked Steven's hair. "You are a good son and a fine young man."

Steven abruptly changed the subject. "Tell me something," he said. "How did you stand being chained down there in the darkness for so long?"

"Faith. Faith and nothing else."

"Weren't you ever afraid?"

"Absolutely, yes. Many times," Emma said. "And lonely and angry and sad."

"How did you cope with all those feelings?"

"I had a little trick for that. Every time I felt one of those things creeping into my heart, I pictured it as big scoops of pralines and cream ice cream piled on top of a chocolate fudge brownie. And then I ate it all up! I have heard that the demon you swallow gives you its power."

"Hey, I like that," Steven said. "But speaking of ice cream, what did you eat down there? How did you survive?"

"Remember the water that was dripping into that pool in the cavern? The Great Serpent put that there to sustain me. He enriched the water with every nutrient needed for human survival, and made it so that the water streamed in and out without ceasing. You see, his desire was not to kill me, but to keep me alive and suffering for eternity."

"Were you ever tempted to refuse the water and let yourself die?" Steven asked, and then quickly backtracked. "I'm sorry, that's a morbid thing to ask."

"No, I never considered it," Emma said. "Remember what I said about faith? Some surrender when they face adversity, but not me. I choose to be one of those people who finds a way, even in the face of great obstacles."

"I hope I can have that kind of faith and power," Steven said.

"Oh, you already have them. You're just not fully aware of it yet. You are very brave."

"Not really," Steven said. "Most of the time I'm pretty afraid."

"Ah, but you go on anyway," Emma said. "And that is the definition of true courage."

Steven shrugged and said, "I just do what anybody would do."

"Have you heard the expression 'The Mistake who would become the Savior'?"

Steven rolled his eyes. "Yes, I've heard it."

"I take it that you do not believe it," Emma observed.

"I don't know what it means."

"Well, it certainly beats what they call me," Emma said. "The Mistake with No End."

"But why? Why would anyone say that about you?"

"I do not know," Emma answered. "But I have learned that it is usually much easier for others to see us for what we truly are than it is for us to see ourselves. Do you understand?"

"Yes, I think so," Steven said.

"So perhaps as we spend time together and you get to know me, you will see the truth of my prophecy just as I see the truth of yours."

"I have to say...you are very intelligent for a..." Steven began. "How old are you, anyway?"

"I suppose it depends on your perspective," Emma said. "I was about your age when I left The Before. But I'm not really sure how to measure how long I've been here. A day, a week or a year? Or perhaps it's been a thousand years."

"A thousand years?" Steven exclaimed.

"Give or take a thousand. Like I said, I'm not sure."

"But you're so very young and beau--" Steven flushed bright red.

"Don't be embarrassed. I think you are quite handsome as well. Many who come to The After do not age at all. They remain exactly as they were on the day they arrived. Although for others, that is not the case, and I do not know why. That is a mystery governed by Big Father."

"Oh, yeah, I keep hearing about Big Father," Steven said skeptically. "Have you ever met him?"

Emma giggled and her dimples lit up, and it set Steven's heart racing. "Not likely, silly," she said. "And I've never known anyone who has."

"Let me ask you this," Steven said. "What or where is this After place?"

"It's the level above The Before, and just below The Beyond. Many living things come directly to The After when they pass on from The Before. It's a sort of stopping-off place on the journey of one's existence."

"Did you say 'pass on'? As in, *die*?"

"Yes, but die is not really an accurate description. It is more--"

Steven jumped to his feet, incredulous. "Hold on just a minute. Are you trying to tell me that I'm dead?"

"I am saying that you passed over from The Before."

"Dead."

"If that is how you persist in viewing it," Emma said.

"Well, I don't believe it," Steven said defiantly. He began to pace back and forth along the ledge. "I don't look or feel dead. I wasn't dead when I knocked Volpe off his horse, was I? I wasn't dead when I fought those wolves and snakes. And I was very much alive when I crawled through that awful cave and rescued you!"

"You knocked Volpe off his horse?" Emma interrupted.

Steven ignored her and ranted on, "All along I've figured this was just some elaborate dream, a nightmare, and that I'd wake up from it eventually. Or that maybe I'd gotten sick and was delusional with fever. Or that maybe somebody, like that jerk Roger Hobson, slipped something into my lunch or my energy drink, and I was hallucinating--"

Suddenly, Emma kissed Steven on the lips. It was brief and light as a feather, but a kiss nonetheless. Steven's eyes went wide as the moon over the Ooljee, and

116

he fell immediately silent, staring at the pretty blonde girl before him.

"Why…what was that for?" Steven stuttered.

"I thought it might be the only way to get you to stop talking."

"Well, at least now I know for sure I'm not dead."

Chapter 22

Steven Standing followed Emma Free down the cliff under the cover of darkness. There were stars twinkling in the sky – it was the first time Steven had seen stars since arriving in The After – and the air was crisp and cool. The sky here was no longer an eerie aquamarine as it had been above the After City and the Ooljee Forest. Rather, it was more like the sky Steven knew back home, although he couldn't spot any of the familiar constellations – the Dippers, the Seven Sisters, Orion.

"We must be as quiet as possible," Emma whispered as they reached the jungle floor and crouched behind a large boulder. "Stay low to the ground and keep your eyes and ears fully alert. There are many dangers here."

Steven tightened the pack on his back and clutched The Ripper firmly in his right hand. It gave off a soft white glow.

"That light will give us away," Emma said. "You must darken it for now, but keep your weapon ever at the ready."

Steven focused on the bat, willed it to go dark, and it obeyed. "Cool," Steven said. "It still blows my mind how it does that."

Emma shushed Steven and motioned for him to follow her on hands and knees beneath long rows of bulky plants with leaves the size of elephant ears. They traveled this way, in fits and starts for many hours, through thickets of sticky ferns, prickly stalks, and winding vines. Every so often they paused and listened intently, their ears gradually growing attuned to the strange sounds of the Geni Jungle. There were squawks, squeals, and chatter from unseen creatures, and odd gnawing and crunching noises in the darkness.

As daylight was breaking, they came upon a very narrow gully, thick with high grass and brilliant flowers of every color in the rainbow. Still crawling, they followed the tight ravine as it sloped downward toward a clearing.

Suddenly something sharp and cold cut Steven's palm. There, half-buried in the soil beneath him, was the jagged edge of an object eggshell white in color, now glistening with his fresh, red blood.

"Hey, look at this," Steven whispered, digging into the dirt. "Ugh, it looks like…a skull…a human skull."

"Quickly, wipe the blood away and wrap your wound in something," Emma said.

"Why? It's not that bad; it's just a little cut."

"But the scent of blood will carry most swiftly on the wind," Emma warned. "It may bring company we most definitely do not want."

Steven did as she asked and they moved on quickly, finding more skulls – some human, some not – and a variety of other bones along the way. Where the crevasse opened into the edge of the clearing, they came upon a large pile of skulls with gruesome grimaces forever frozen on their fearsome faces. Steven felt as though the hollow eye sockets were staring him down, unblinking, unrelenting, looking through him and into Eternity.

"Uh, I don't like the looks of this at all," Steven said.

"There are many predators here," Emma said. "The Geni Jungle is quite different from the Ooljee Forest."

"Ya know, I see these skulls and I've heard all the sounds here in the jungle, but I've yet to see one living creature," Steven observed. "Weird, isn't it?"

Emma nodded. "Yes, weird, indeed, but good. Let us hope our luck will hold."

Steven peered out from the coppice into the clearing. "So, what now?"

Emma studied the scene, sniffed the air, and listened intently. "I think we should stay here in this secluded spot and wait once more for darkness. That open area would be much too dangerous to try to cross in the daylight."

"Fine with me; my knees are raw from all this crawling," Steven said, reclining against his backpack. "And my hands are too sore to rub my knees with."

"Stop complaining," Emma said. "Would you prefer to end up like those poor souls in that pile of bones?"

"What difference would it make?" Steven asked with a smirk. "According to you, I'm already dead anyway."

"I must say that I am surprised that you've said nothing more on that subject until now," Emma said.

"Like I told you, that's because I don't believe it."

"Fine," Emma said. "Believe what you want."

Not wanting to argue, Steven kept quiet for a while. He picked up a twig and drew in the dirt. First he sketched a large circle with a myriad of odd shapes and figures inside it. Then he drew a line through the middle of the circle, cutting it in half, followed by another line which quartered it, and two more lines which split it into eight pieces.

Mystified, Emma said, "It looks like some sort of symbolic representation of the spiritual realm."

Steven smiled.

"Is it meant to depict the fragmentation of the cosmos?"

"No," Steven replied.

"Well, what is it, then?"

"A pizza," Steven said. "Could you conjure one up with your magic? I'm starving."

"I cannot afford to waste my energies on something so trivial."

"Trivial? You've obviously never had a deep dish pizza with the works." Steven closed his eyes and licked his lips. "Man, a pizza would be so perfect right now. Pepperoni, cheese, mushrooms, banana peppers--"

Emma put a hand over Steven's mouth and said, "Shh, listen. I hear something."

Steven suddenly realized that the jungle had gone silent. "I don't hear anything at all. Not a single sound. What's up with that?"

"Something is coming," Emma whispered.

Then Steven heard screams and shouts in the distance, growing steadily closer, though he could not determine what was being said. Then came the sounds of running footsteps, rustling brush, and branches being broken. Suddenly a short, hairy creature burst forth from the undergrowth on the opposite side of the clearing and out into the open.

"It's a Brisbane," Steven said excitedly, about to jump up. "They're friends of mine."

"No, be still," Emma said, holding him down. "We best stay hidden."

Although the Brisbane was nearly forty yards away, Steven could tell that the creature was frantic and terrified of someone, or some*thing*. Surprised by the open expanse of the clearing, the Brisbane hesitated, assessing his options, uncertain where to go next. But before he could move, his pursuers stormed out of the jungle and surrounded him.

121

Steven swallowed hard as he watched six strange, pig-like beings circle the Brisbane. They stood upright on cloven hooves at the ends of long, knobby legs; and they reminded Steven of bristle-haired boars that he'd once hunted with his father and uncles. But these beasts were far more fearsome, each with a pair of tusks more than a foot long, set on either side of a long, pink snout. They seemed to be toying with the Brisbane now, moving around him, making snorting and slurping sounds, with long strands of saliva oozing from their nasty, pig mouths.

"What are they going to do?" Steven whispered.

"I assume they intend to devour him," Emma said softly.

The Brisbane hissed and shouted at the pig-men in fear and defiance, but they merely laughed at him.

"We've got to try to help him," Steven pleaded.

"No, we cannot," Emma said firmly. "It's too late."

Suddenly one of the creatures leaped upon the Brisbane and ran its tusks straight through the poor fellow's skull. Then, with its victim fully impaled upon its sharp horns, the pig-man lifted him high into the air and roared with delight. The Brisbane hung there on the end of the tusks, legs and arms jerking and twisting as his life-blood poured out of the holes in his head and splattered about on the ground. The other boar-like monsters rushed in quickly to lap up the blood from the dirt, while the murderous pig-man thrust his snout into the Brisbane's head and sucked out the brain.

"Me like brains!" the creature snorted as he slung the body to the side. The other five pig-men leaped upon the carcass and ravenously tore the flesh from the bones.

Steven felt bile rise up in his throat and he gagged involuntarily. The brain-eating pig-man spun around and stared toward where Steven and Emma lay hidden at the edge of the jungle thicket. Steven could see the pig-man's black, beady eyes peering into the thicket, and his long, whiskered snout crinkling as he sniffed the air.

"I'm so sorry," Steven breathed.

"No matter," Emma whispered. "They would likely have caught our scent eventually. We might as well deal with them now as later. At least this way, we have a slight advantage."

"How so?" Steven asked.

"We can see them but they do not yet see us. We must strike now."

"I agree completely," Steven said. "Maybe if I can take down one of them, the others will scatter."

"Perhaps," Emma said doubtfully.

Steven gripped The Ripper with both hands, closed his eyes and concentrated. When the bat surged with power, Steven leaped out of the jungle and pointed it toward the nearest pig-man. A bolt of blue-white energy sizzled from the bat and struck the creature squarely in the chest. The pig-man fell to the ground, smoldering and squealing. Steven thought he smelled bacon.

But the other pig-men did not run. Instead, they surrounded Steven quickly, snarling, snorting and circling just as they had done with the Brisbane.

"Uh, so much for that idea," Steven said to Emma, who was still hid in the bushes. Steven turned quickly from side to side, maintaining a defensive posture in the center of the circle, holding The Ripper out threateningly toward the beasts, but they seemed oblivious to the danger.

"They must be very brave," Steven said.

"Or maybe they are just extremely stupid," Emma shouted loudly.

The pig-men turned toward the jungle, now aware that Steven apparently had a partner hidden in the thicket.

"Run!" Emma said to Steven. "Get out of the circle!"

Steven dashed between two of the distracted pig-men and toward the jungle as Emma stood and spoke:

Cereal and milk, milk and cereal;
Bind these pigs with bonds ethereal.

Yellow wisps of smoke and sparkles of light danced from Emma's fingertips and closed tightly around the legs and arms of the pig-men. They lost their balance and fell to the ground, squealing and struggling to free themselves from the supernatural bindings.

"Man, that was so cool," Steven said as he and Emma ran across the clearing.

"That will hold them for a while, but more are coming. I can hear them. We must hurry to the Zero Line," Emma said as they plunged into the jungle. Once they were hidden from sight, she fell to her knees.

"What's wrong? Are you okay?" Steven asked. "You don't look so good."

"That was a very difficult and powerful spell, but I think I can make it."

Steven reached down to help her. "Let me carry you."

"No, I do not want to be a burden," Emma said, pushing him away. "Go ahead without me, and I will try to keep up."

"Are you crazy? I'm not leaving you behind."

There were sounds of thudding hooves and frenzied snorts in the clearing as a troop of at least thirty pig-men arrived and discovered their incapacitated comrades.

"You will not make it if you carry me," Emma said.

"Yes, I will. I bet you don't even weigh ninety pounds." And with that, Steven lifted her up and ran, tearing wildly through the jungle, leaping over fallen trees, jumping small ravines, pushing through thick brush. Even amid all the chaos and danger, Emma was so drained by the casting of the spell that she fell immediately into a deep sleep in his arms.

Steven could hear the rabid shrieks of their pursuers who were caught up in the thrill of the hunt, driven by bloodlust and the desire to feast on human brains. His heart was pounding like a jackhammer, adrenaline was flooding his system, and his feet seemed to barely touch the ground as he ran. Bursting through a dense coppice, he lost his footing as the ground suddenly dropped away. Steven slid, stumbled, and tumbled down a long, steep hillside through heavy foliage, all the while struggling to cradle Emma in his arms and keep his rucksack from being ripped from his back. Finally, he slipped off a small outcropping and dropped ten feet into a thicket beside a raging river.

Concealed in the brush, Steven lay on his back trying to catch his breath. There were clumps of dirt in his hair, scratches all over his body, and leaves and sticks stuck in his clothing. Emma, however, was still asleep against his chest, having come through the entire unpleasant experience virtually unscathed. Her eyelids fluttered open and she looked up at Steven and whispered, "Did I miss anything exciting?"

Steven smiled, impulsively kissed her on the forehead, and then blushed brightly.

Emma furrowed her brow and asked, "Why is there a twig stuck in your ear?"

Chapter 23

Steven Standing was exhausted, beaten, battered and nearing his wits' end. He knew the pig-men would soon be on their trail, but he had an overwhelming need to close his eyes, if only for a moment. He lay back in the brush and sleep pushed in upon him. Deeper and deeper he drifted...until he heard someone calling his name and felt someone shaking him. It was Emma Free trying to wake him and bring him back to the present.

"Steven, Steven, you can't sleep now. The pig-men will be here soon," Emma said. "We need a plan quickly...or a miracle."

"Wh...what?...oh...I'm sorry," Steven said groggily. "I guess I was out of it there for a minute."

"Perhaps you really did hit your head," Emma suggested, picking dirt and twigs from his hair.

"Maybe, but I'll be okay," Steven said, sitting up and rubbing his eyes. "Just let me think for a minute."

Desperately hoping a brilliant idea would strike him, Steven grabbed a long plant stem of some sort and chewed on it nervously. The taste was bitter and made his mouth tingle. He stopped and stared at the strange plant before him. It looked familiar somehow with yellow leaf pads, long stalks, and small orange flowers.

Realization swept over him. "The Succato! This is the plant she told me about," Steven said. "We may have found our miracle."

"What?" Emma said, looking from Steven to the plant and back to Steven. "What are you talking about?"

"I'm really not sure," Steven answered as he dug into the dark, rich soil around the roots of the Succato. "I just have a feeling."

There were vicious hog calls and thundering hooves now echoing down the hillside toward them. Steven and Emma were well hidden in the thicket next to the river, but eventually the pig-men would pick up their scent and discover them. It was only a matter of time.

"I don't know what you are doing," Emma said. "But I suggest you do it quickly."

"Here, eat this," Steven said, holding out a handful of loam.

Emma looked at his offering and scrunched up her face. "*That* is your plan? Eat dirt? You really did hit your head."

"Just trust me. Alexia told me about this plant and the soil beneath it."

The pig-men were getting closer and closer, snarling and shrieking, *Me want brains, me want brains!* Emma nodded and whispered, "Okay, Steven, I will trust you."

Steven took a bite from the lump of soil in his palm and Emma followed his lead. Grimacing at the disagreeable taste and texture on their palates and trying not to gag, they swallowed three dollops apiece of the gritty substance.

"Now what?" Emma asked.

"I don't know," Steven replied.

"Some plan," Emma said, her words as dry as dirt.

"Let's concentrate on what we want," Steven suggested.

"Well, I know what we do *not* want," Emma said. "We do not want those creatures to find us."

"True. We want to be hidden from their sight. Focus on that thought."

"I am…feeling rather…weird," Emma said.

"Wow, you look weird, too." Right before his eyes, Emma was turning the very color of the soil they'd eaten.

"So do you," Emma whispered. "This is…most strange."

Steven faintly saw Emma speaking but her words became jumbled and dreamlike in his ears. In fact, everything seemed to be slipping into an alternate reality or dimension. His skin felt grainy and his blood thick. He had the sensation that the ground was swallowing him up, or that he and his possessions were somehow melting into the soil. He watched with wonder as Emma also transformed and became one with the dirt, blended into the ground as if she no longer existed. They were hidden from their attackers!

Soon the pig-men reached the spot where Steven and Emma had been only a few moments before, and still were, in a sense. Sniffing and snorting, they followed the human scent to where it ended there at the edge of the roiling river rapids.

"They fall down hill in water," one of the pig-men said. The others agreed.

"Water carry them that way," one said, pointing.

"They drown," another said.

"Still be brains to eat!" the first pig-man said. "Who finds first gets brains!"

Energized by fresh thoughts of their favorite delicacy, the troop of pig-men rumbled down the riverbank, hoping to find human bodies washed up somewhere along the shore. As their enthusiastic oinks faded in the distance, the effects of the enchanted soil began to wear off. Steven and Emma were pushed up gently by the dirt, reappearing *from* the dirt, and lay wide-eyed and astonished on the ground.

"Wow," Steven whispered.

"Wow," Emma agreed. "I could almost feel them walk right over top of us."

"So, where do we go now?" Steven asked.

"We must cross that river."

Steven looked out across the raging waters and gulped. "Uh, you've got to be kidding. Even the best swimmer in the world couldn't get across that. Even if we had a boat, it would get smashed on the rocks in a few seconds."

Emma stood with hands on hips and studied the hurdle before them. The opposite side of the river was a completely different terrain from where they were – it was rocky and barren with very little plant life, almost like a desert.

"See those huge boulders over there lining the riverbank?" Emma asked. "On the other side of those should be the Zero Line and the Mirror Land I told you about."

"Isn't there a bridge or some other way across?" Steven asked.

"Yes, there are two crossing points that I know of," Emma answered. "But they are many miles upriver. It would take us a long time to get there, and we would be in constant danger from the pig-men and other predators in the Geni Jungle."

"I have an idea," Steven said.

"Does it involve eating dirt?" Emma asked.

"No, but it does involve the Succato." Steven pulled off one of the plant's leaf pads, the size of a loaf of bread, and carefully tore a small hole in it for drinking. He scrunched up his nose at the smell emanating from inside, and looked hesitantly at Emma.

"Another of the She-Wolf's suggestions, I suppose," Emma said.

Steven nodded, still grimacing. "Yep. And I have a feeling this might taste worse than the dirt, if that's possible."

He put his mouth to the opening and tipped the leaf up with both hands. A thick, greenish goo similar to a mixture of curdled milk and slurried cabbage oozed out of the hole and onto Steven's tongue.

"You are a braver man than I," Emma laughed.

Steven tried not to think about the sticky substance, but rather to simply swallow it down as fast as possible. "Yuuuuuuccckkkk," he said as it almost came back up.

"How will that get us across the river?" Emma asked.

"Alexia said the liquid in the Succato plant would give me power over plant life for a short time. Let's see if my idea will work."

Steven studied the trees around them, picked out the tallest one, and wrapped his arms around it. He judged that, if it were lying horizontally, it would easily reach across the river. For several minutes, Steven hugged the great tree tightly and concentrated with all his mental energy.

"I don't understand," Emma said. "How is that going to--"

Steven shushed her softly and whispered, "Just give me a little more time. I feel something happening."

Slowly, the massive plant began to groan and creak as though it were waking from a long slumber. Steven clung to the tree as it strained, stretched and bent – almost to its breaking point – ever so slowly downward and across the river, reaching out for the opposite shore.

"Amazing," Emma whispered, her eyes wet with tears. "I have never seen such an incredible sight. The tree obeyed you willingly and now provides us a bridge across the treacherous waters."

Steven clung to the tree and did not move, did not reply.

"Steven, are you alright?" Emma asked. "Steven?" She rushed to his side and found him in a trance so intense that his fingers had dug into the bark of the tree. It took all her strength to pry him free and rouse him from his stupor.

"Man, that was awesome," Steven said when he came back to his senses. "I could *feel* the tree all the way from its roots to its leaves. It was like I was inside there where the sap is running, thinking tree thoughts."

"What a spectacular creature," Emma said, running her hand gently along the bark. Then, turning to Steven, she added, "And so are you, my friend, so are you."

Steven blushed and nervously said, "Well, we'd probably better get going. I don't know how long the tree will stay this way."

They made their way carefully along the trunk, weaving through branches and clusters of leaves while the waters raged only a few feet below them, smashing against the rocks and sending up a mist and spray that soaked Steven and Emma to the bone. One misstep could send them plunging to certain destruction.

"Watch out for that limb," Steven said, pointing down. "It's pretty shaky and close to breaking, I think."

"If it held you, I am sure it can hold me," Emma said, then added, "But thank you for being so thoughtful. I will be careful."

When they reached the other side, they jumped off their temporary bridge onto a boulder on the riverbank and surveyed the sight before them.

Just beyond the rocks was a row of twelve wooden crosses, standing tall against the sky. One cross was empty, but the other eleven bore the remains of creatures – some appeared to have been human, others not – that had apparently been crucified perhaps not so long ago. What was left of their rotting, blackened carcasses sagged against the spikes that impaled them, bones protruding and innards leaking out here and there.

Steven and Emma stared with eyes wide and said nothing.

The terrain beyond the crosses was completely flat with a thin layer of white sand barely covering the dark, glistening surface below, like grains of salt poured upon a smooth, black table top. The flat land stretched only a very short distance – not even a hundred feet – to where it was bounded by a shimmering, undulating wall of gelatin-like energy that rose from the floor of the Mirror Land and stretched upward and outward in every direction as far as Steven's eyes could see.

"That wall is the Zero Line," Emma said.

Finally, Steven found his voice, "Well, I thought I'd seen it all since coming to this nightmare place, but I was obviously wrong."

Suddenly there were shouts from the jungle side of the river. The pig-men were back and were scrambling across the tree bridge in pursuit of Steven and Emma.

"Uh, oh," Steven said.

"Uh, oh is correct," Emma said. "Do you have any suggestions for our next course of action?"

Steven gave Emma a dumb look. "I was hoping you would," he said, pulling The Ripper from his backpack. "I guess we fight. Again."

The first of the pig-men was nearly across the river when, with no warning whatsoever, the tree moaned and trembled as though something terrible was happening inside it. As the tremors intensified, some of the pig-men lost their footing and fell into the raging river, while the others hesitated, uncertain of what to do. Suddenly the massive tree shot up to its normal, upright position, snapping back with tremendous velocity just as a branch snaps back after you've pushed it aside when walking through the woods. The sheer force and speed of it slung the remaining, two dozen pig-men a thousand feet up into the air; and sent them soaring across the sky, squealing in terror, deep into the Geni Jungle, never to be seen again.

"Well, that's something you don't see every day," Emma observed.

"For sure," Steven laughed. "Now I can *definitely* say I've seen it all."

Chapter 24

Steven Standing sat down on a rock and rubbed his sore shoulder, the one that had been bitten by the wolves, the same one that he'd landed upon when falling down the tunnel in the Chasm of Caves.

"You are hurting," Emma said. "Perhaps I could conjure some type of healing spell, or at least something to lessen the pain."

"Like Coach always says, I'll just have to suck it up," Steven said. "Besides, you need your strength for what might be ahead."

"Perhaps the worst is over," Emma suggested, and then quickly recanted. "I do not even know why those words came out of my mouth."

"I wondered what you were thinking," Steven laughed.

From behind them came a clattering sound like nails scraping on a Formica tabletop. Steven and Emma spun around to see a giant, bug-like creature scrambling across the rocks toward them. It had more legs than they could count.

"Wow, that thing looks like some kind of humongous, mutated hellgrammite," Steven said.

"A what?"

"A hellgrammite. They're big, scary-looking bugs that my dad used to fish with when I was a boy. I hated those things. One of them bit me once and it hurt like crazy."

"I fear the bite of this one will hurt much more," Emma said.

As the creature came closer, Steven could see that it looked less like a bug and more like a lab experiment gone terribly wrong. In addition to its insect legs and body, it also had crab claws, elephant tusks, a vulture's beak, a scorpion's tail, and a partially veiled human head.

"Now I know what this is," Emma said. "It is called the Chindi-Var. I have heard stories of it."

The Chindi-Var moved toward Steven and he pointed The Ripper at it. White-hot energy sizzled from the end of the bat and struck the monster in the chest. The creature shuddered but kept coming. Steven began to panic.

"Perhaps magical powers of that sort do not work on this enemy," Emma said.

"No kidding," Steven said, leaping over a boulder to escape the attack of the Chindi-Var. But he wasn't quite quick enough and the razor-sharp edge of the beast's snapping claw sliced across his back. Steven cried out in pain as he spun away and dove for cover.

In order to draw the beast away from Steven, Emma pelted it from behind with large stones. When one struck the creature in the head, it squeaked as if in severe pain and turned on Emma viciously. She ducked into a narrow crevice with the Chindi-Var in close pursuit.

"Maybe you found its weak spot," Steven shouted as he pulled a baseball from his backpack and took aim. *I can nail a runner at the plate from deep in the hole at short, so I know I can do this. I bet I can take it down with one perfectly placed throw.*

Steven fired the baseball with all his might and drilled the creature in the back of the head at the base of its skull. The Chindi-Var squealed and staggered for a moment, then recovered and roared with fury.

"Or maybe not," Steven said.

When the Chindi-Var turned around, its face was no longer veiled, and it was smiling.

Now it was Steven's turn to be staggered. He gasped, squeezed his eyes closed, and looked again. "What? No, no, no," he stammered, backing up against a boulder.

The Chindi-Var spoke with the voice of a frail, old woman, "Steven, come here to Grandma. Give Grandma a hug, Steven. Give me some sugar." The voice, the eyes, the face all belonged to Steven's dead grandmother. And he could not look away.

"It's not real, Steven. That is not your grandmother," Emma shouted. "Look away and break its hold over you! You must look away!"

But Steven couldn't take his eyes off that face. He was paralyzed, helpless, dead meat, as the Chindi-Var approached him with a tusk aimed at his throat.

From the rocks above, there came a blur of brown and black flashing through the air. Like a canine missile of vengeance, Bang slammed into the Chindi-Var's shoulder and slashed into the soft spot of the creature's neck, ripping open its jugular vein. Blood spurted ten feet into the air and the Chindi-Var made gurgling sounds and spun in circles with Bang clinging to its back.

In desperation, the Chindi-Var reached blindly back over its head with its crab claws, snapping at its canine attacker, and stabbed wildly and repeatedly with its scorpion tail, finally striking Bang in the leg. The dog cried out in pain and fell to the ground where the Chindi-Var tried to crush him underfoot, even as its own life-blood was pouring out in the dirt.

Steven screamed out in horror, "No!!!!!!!"

With a frightening roar, Nina Nita rushed to Bang's aid. Even though the Chindi-Var was several feet taller than him, the angry bear plowed into the big bug, knocked it to the ground, and slashed it with his mighty claws, again and again, until it moved no more.

"You hurt Steven Standing's dog," Nina Nita said. "You won't never hurt nobody else ever again."

With the Chindi-Var's spell broken, Steven rushed to Bang's side, fell to his knees, and swept his faithful friend into his arms. Bang nuzzled weakly against Steven's chest, and boy and dog wept together. "You saved us," Steven said softly. "You saved our lives. And now...and now..."

Bang whimpered and quivered from head to tail as the poison slowly spread through his body.

Steven looked up at Emma with tears streaming down his face. "Please, we...we've got to do...something," he stuttered. "Can you help him? Isn't there some spell you can use? Please...help him..."

"I don't know," Emma said uncertainly. "I can manipulate objects or sometimes alter situations, but I have never healed living tissue with my powers."

"You've got to try," Steven pleaded. "Please try."

Emma locked eyes with Steven and something passed between them, something neither of them had ever known before.

"Yes, I will try," Emma said, and she lay her hands gently upon Bang's bloody wound.

Chapter 25

"Steven Standing, you and your companions are quite a fascinating and impressive band of visitors to my humble abode," a voice called out.

Startled, Steven and Emma looked up from their wounded friend. "Who said that?" Steven asked, looking all around. "Where did that come from?"

A gust of wind whipped up a salty sheen on the surface of the Mirror Land, and from it came the sound of one pair of hands clapping slowly, followed by the buzzing of a small motor. The puzzled comrades peered into the cloud of dust, waiting for the speaker to reveal himself.

From the midst of the miniature maelstrom appeared a little old man in a fully accessorized, motorized wheelchair. The elderly gentleman was conservatively dressed in what appeared to be his Sunday-go-to-meetin' clothes – a dark, neatly pressed suit, crisp white shirt, skinny black tie, and shiny dress shoes. His face and hands were wrinkled with age, his hair white, and he had a crooked grin on his face as he zipped toward them in his chair.

"If only you could see your faces," the old man laughed. "You are indeed the epitome of bewilderment at this moment. Ah, wait just a minute…you actually *can* see your faces…if I do *this*."

He retrieved an old-fashioned Polaroid camera from the small storage container on the side of his wheelchair, pointed it at them, and said, "Say 'cheeeeese'." And then he snapped their picture. In a moment, the photograph popped out and the smiling man held it up before them. "See? There you are in all your glory."

"Sir, I don't know who you are," Steven said. "But we don't have time for this right now. My dog is badly injured."

"My apologies. I was not aware," the man said as he motored toward them. "Please, allow me to help."

Emma eyed him warily. "Something about this stranger makes me very uncomfortable," she whispered to Steven. "We don't know who he is or anything about him."

"I don't *care* who he is if he can save Bang," Steven said.

"My name is Scranius Olbaid, and my hearing is very sharp," the man said gruffly, looking at Emma. "Please place the dog up here on my lap."

Steven did as he asked. Scranius leaned over Bang, put his mouth upon the wound, and sucked hard and long.

Steven grimaced and said, "What are you doing?"

The man raised his head from the whimpering dog and answered with blood-soaked lips, "I am sucking the poison from his canine body."

"Hadn't you better spit the poison out?" Nina Nita asked, peering over the old man's shoulder. "Poison is very bad for you."

Scranius looked up at the bear, arched an eyebrow sharply, and said, "I assure you, Mr. Bear, I am immune to the venom of the Chindi-Var."

When he was finished, Scranius took a fresh, white handkerchief from his breast pocket, unfolded it carefully, and blotted his mouth dry. Then he took some ointment and bandages from the supply box on his wheelchair, and handed them to Emma. "Young lady, please dress the dog's wound with these."

139

Not fond of taking orders, Emma hesitated; but, feeling Steven's eyes upon her, she complied and tended to Bang's injury.

Scranius continued, "He will need to rest at least for a day, but I predict he will soon be bounding about, doing whatever it is that dogs do."

"Thank you, sir, thank you so very much for saving Bang's life," Steven said. "That crazy old mutt means the world to me."

"It was my pleasure to be of assistance," Scranius said. "All of you are welcome to stay here as he recuperates. In fact, you may stay for as long as you wish. I could certainly use some assistance in running this place."

"You don't strike me as someone who needs anyone's help," Raven observed. "I suspect you are quite capable of most anything."

"Well, then, perhaps it is your company I seek," Scranius said, smiling widely. "I do get rather lonely here all by myself."

The old man's hands trembled with a barely discernible tremor, and Steven found himself feeling sorry him. He couldn't quite pinpoint the reason, but there was something about Scranius that reminded Steven of his own grandfather, although this man was obviously much more eccentric and sophisticated, and with an air of mystery and danger about him.

"I am curious about something," Emma said. "I thought this was the domain of the Great Serpent."

"The Great Serpent? I have seen no serpents here, I'm afraid," Scranius said. "There's just little old me."

"What's with all these crosses? Who crucified those poor souls?" Raven asked.

"You are certainly an inquisitive and talkative fowl, but unfortunately, I don't have answers to your questions," Scranius said. "Those crosses were here when I arrived."

"And why is one of them empty?" Emma asked.

"I suppose that's for the one that got away," Scranius laughed.

"Or perhaps it is simply yet to be filled," Emma said.

"Perhaps," Scranius said coldly. Then turning to the others he said, "You must be hungry. You have probably had nothing but grubs for days. You may as well eat while you wait for your friend to recover."

"Yeah, I'm really hungry," Nina Nita said.

"Yes, but you're *always* hungry," Raven cawed.

"If Mr. Bear is hungry, Mr. Bear should eat," Scranius said, and a large barrel of honey appeared before him instantly. "Now, eat and enjoy!"

Nina Nita looked at the barrel dumbfounded. "How'd you do that?"

"You do like honey, don't you?" Scranius asked. "I can take it away, if you wish."

The bear shouted *No,* plunged his face into the barrel, and began lapping up the thick, golden goo. As Nina Nita feasted, Scranius waved his hand and a worm-blackberry pie appeared before Raven, a bowl of mutton stew before Emma, and a loaded, deep-dish pizza materialized in front of Steven.

"Wow!" Steven said, digging in. "This is like an answer to prayer."

"Indeed. Now, when was the last time any of you slept in a comfortable bed?" Scranius asked.

"When's the last time we slept at all?" Steven retorted with a mouthful of pizza.

Scranius snapped his fingers and luxurious beds appeared for each of them. "Why not rest here for a time, nourish yourselves and consider my offer while your dog

141

recovers? Surely you would not want him to travel until he's fully healed."

Steven plopped down on one of the beds with a slice of pizza in each hand. "I guess you do have a point there, Mr. Olbaid."

"Please, no need for such formality," the man in the wheelchair said. "I insist you call me Scranius."

"Sorry, it's just the way I was raised," Steven said. "My mom and dad taught me to always respect my elders."

"Oh, how wonderful they must be," Scranius said. "Do you have a picture of them?"

A look of sadness swept over Steven's face. "Yes, I have a bunch of pictures...or, at least, I did." He pulled his cellphone from his backpack. "They're all on here but I can't access them. Dead battery."

"Perhaps I can help," Scranius said, taking the phone from Steven. He sifted through items in his supply box until he found what he sought. "Ah, ha! This cable should do the trick." Scranius plugged the cord into the phone and connected it to the power supply on his motorized wheelchair. In a moment, the phone buzzed to life.

"Awesome!" Steven shouted. "Thank you for this, for everything, Mr. Olbaid."

"Please...Scranius, if you would," the old man said.

"Okay, then...Scranius," Steven said, as he scrolled excitedly through the photo albums contained on his phone. "I can't thank you enough. You don't know how much this means to me."

"Oh, but I think I do."

Chapter 26

Steven Standing lay on his back upon the plush bed provided by Scranius Olbaid, with his cell phone and The Ripper clutched tightly to his chest, and pizza sauce on his chin. His faithful dog, Bang, was resting beside him, having dined on soft doggie biscuits and warm broth. Both were fast asleep, even with Nina Nita's snoring, sleeping more comfortably than they had in a very long time. That is, until Emma sat down on the edge of the bed.

"Steven, Steven…" Emma whispered.

Steven groaned and rolled over on his side.

"Steven, are you awake?"

"Yes, of course," Steven answered dryly. "I'm wide awake. Can't you tell?"

"I do not trust him."

"What? Who?"

"You know who," Emma said.

"Scranius?"

"Scranius," Emma said, spitting the word out as one might spit out a gristle of meat.

"Why not?"

Emma stared into the undulating gelatin wall known as the Zero Line, thinking. "I do not know," she answered at last.

"Well, that's ridiculous," Steven said. "He's done nothing but help us. He fed us and gave us a warm bed. And don't forget, he saved Bang's life."

"Yes, yes," Emma said slowly. "But why? Why did he do all these things?"

"Maybe because he's a good person."

"Perhaps. But don't you think he's rather…odd?"

"Well, you're not exactly the Queen of Normal," Steven joked.

As if on patrol, Scranius had been continuously motoring slowly up and down the long strip of land between the river and the Zero Line wall. Now he was coming back toward them once again, passing along in front of the row of crosses, his wheels rolling easily over the razor-thin layer of sand atop the smooth surface of the Mirror Land.

"Look at him," Steven said. "He's just a little old man in a wheelchair. I kinda feel sorry for him."

"I do not think he needs our pity. There is more to him than meets the eye," Emma said. "How did he make these beds and the food appear from thin air?"

"He must have powers like you," Steven explained. "Why is that so hard to believe?"

Raven hopped over and alit beside them on the super-deluxe bed. "I too have questions. How did Olbaid suck out and swallow the poison from Bang's body without it harming him? And what did he do with the carcass of the Chindi-Var?" the bird queried. "He is most strange, indeed. I agree with Miss Emma; I say we err on the side of caution with this old man."

"Yeah, I agree that he's pretty weird, and that part about the poison really gives me the creeps," Steven conceded. "But still, he's done so much for us and hasn't threatened us in any way."

"Something else just occurred to me," Emma said. "How did he know your name?"

Steven thought about that for a minute. "Hhmm, you're right. He did call out my name at the very first, didn't he? I was so worried about Bang at the time that I didn't even think about that."

"Mystery upon mystery," Raven said.

"Well, it seems that others have known who I was because of that stupid prophecy," Steven said. "Maybe that's the explanation."

"Here he comes now," Emma said. "Perhaps we should simply ask him."

"Sure, why not?" Steven said, sitting up and swinging his feet over the edge of the bed. As the old man came near, Steven said, "I was just wondering, Scranius, sir, how did you know my name?"

Scranius seemed momentarily taken off-guard by the question, but then he replied, "Why you are most famous indeed. The prophecy, of course, firstly; and secondly, your baseball exploits are known far and wide."

"But I play Little League baseball in New Mexico," Steven said. "I'm not even in college yet. How could--"

Scranius interrupted him, "I am a devoted fan of the national pastime, and I follow it closely at all levels, even Little League. Steven Standing, were it not for your untimely demise, you could have been a star in the Major Leagues. Of this I have no doubt."

Steven was both grateful for and somewhat embarrassed by the praise being heaped upon him. "Well, thanks, Mr. Olbaid, but I don't know about all that," he stammered.

"I am actually planning to construct a baseball field here in the Mirror Land," Scranius said. "Real grass, old-fashioned bleachers, the seventh inning stretch, ballpark hot dogs with mustard and slaw, the whole bit, you know. It's going to be quite marvelous! I could use a star player like you for my team."

"I want a hot dog," Nina Nita said.

"And where are the other players and teams?" Raven asked skeptically. "Who will fill those bleachers?"

Scranius looked askance at the raven. "My, but you are an inquisitive bird, aren't you? I get the feeling you do not believe me."

"Much of what you say does seem a bit fantastical," Emma interjected. "It almost seems as though you are, well, trying too hard."

"Yes, that's it exactly," Raven said.

Suddenly the old man's countenance turned darker, and there was an almost ominous tone to his voice. "I have been a most gracious host, have I not? I have provided for your needs, healed your friend, and asked nothing in return save for your companionship. And yet, you interrogate me as though I were some type of criminal."

"We meant no offense," Emma said.

"We were merely curious," Raven said.

"You know what curiosity did to the cat, do you not?" Scranius said. "Cats are not all that different from birds and little girls."

Emma's jaw tightened and her fair-skinned cheeks flushed bright red as she glared at the old man.

Steven was caught off guard and very uncomfortable with the sudden escalation of tension among his friends. "Emma, please calm down," he said.

"Yeah, why can't we all just get along?" Nina Nita said, sprawled out on his plush, extra-large bed.

"The bear is correct," Scranius said soothingly. "There is no need for hostility here. Let us change the subject."

Scranius Oblaid moved closer to Steven and took the boy's hand in his. "I too am curious about something. Tell me, Steven Standing, what brought you here to the Mirror Land? Are you exploring?"

146

"Not exactly," Steven said. "We are searching for something called the Portal so that I can get back to my life in The Before."

"Oh my, young friend, I hate to be the one to tell you this, but you cannot go back to The Before. No one can."

"But...but I was told that it might be possible if--"

"You have been misinformed, deceived even."

"You are wrong," Emma burst out, unable to hold her tongue any longer. "It most definitely is possible to return to The Before."

"Oh, really?" Scranius said, wheeling his chair back around to face her. "And exactly how does one do that?"

"Through the Portal."

"And where is this Portal you speak of?"

"It's on the other side of that shimmering wall, just beyond the Zero Line."

"How do you know that?" Scranius persisted in his questioning. "Have you seen this so-called Portal?"

Emma hesitated. "Well, no, not yet. But I have heard--"

"You have heard lies," Scranius interrupted. "Even if there was a Portal over there, you could not reach it because no one can pass through the Zero Line. It is a wall of energy designed to destroy interlopers who would attempt to cross it."

"You are the liar!" Emma shouted.

Scranius Olbaid narrowed his eyes, clenched his teeth, and waves of anger seemed to emanate from the top of his head like heat rising off sunbaked blacktop. "It is most impolite to insult your gracious host," he hissed, raising a finger toward Emma. "You should be taught a lesson--"

"Mr. Olbaid...Scranius, sir," Steven said, hoping to diffuse the situation.

Scranius took a deep breath, reined himself in and said calmly, "No worries. The young girl and I differ on this

147

particular topic. We must simply agree to disagree for now."

Chapter 27

Steven Standing stood silently before the wall, considering the words of Scranius Olbaid and peering into the translucent depths of the Zero Line, mesmerized by its shape-shifting clouds and flickering lights.

"What are you doing?" Emma whispered from behind, startling Steven.

"Oh, I'm just thinking..." Steven said softly. "I'm itching to get through this thing, but I'm afraid to try anything until Bang is able to travel. I mean, what if I was to just stick my hand in there to test it out and it sucked me inside?"

"True, it is impossible to predict what might happen when we attempt to cross it," Emma said.

"Maybe you could cast some sort of spell," Steven suggested. "Or maybe I could blow a hole in it with The Ripper."

Emma craned her neck and looked up where the Zero Line's wall of vibrating energy stretched beyond the clouds. "I have never seen anything quite like this wall," she said. "I do not know what to expect from it, and sadly, your friend, Mr. Olbaid, is no help in this regard. He is most definitely keeping something from us."

"Oh, no. Don't start back on that again, Emma," Steven pleaded.

"Surely you must know that he is lying to us," Emma persisted.

"No, I don't know that," Steven argued. "What reason would he have to lie? And if he was a bad guy, why would he be so nice to us?"

"Because my instincts tell me that he does not want us to reach the Portal."

Steven sat down cross-legged and pondered, drawing absently in the sand with his fingers. Emma squatted beside him and they sat in silence for several minutes.

Suddenly Steven snapped his fingers and said, "Hey, I just got an idea. I don't know why I didn't think of it before. Let's see what happens if we throw something in there."

"I don't know..." Emma said.

Steven scooped up a handful of white sand, jumped up, and tossed it into the undulating barrier. As the sand disappeared inside the wall of dark there was a sound like air escaping from a bicycle tire. Suddenly the sand shot back out of the Zero Line with a great burst, stinging Steven's and Emma's faces and burning their eyes.

"Ow! Ow!" they cried out, turning away and rubbing their eyes.

"Maybe that wasn't such a great idea," Steven said, mustering a half-smile.

"You think?" Emma said.

"Fools! I told you the Zero Line could not be penetrated, but you would not listen," Scranius shouted, motoring toward them. "Now move away from there."

"We are not your subjects; we do not have to obey your commands," Emma said.

For a moment Steven thought Scranius Olbaid was going to rise up out of his wheelchair and walk. But once again, he restrained himself, took Steven calmly by the hand and said, "Young Mr. Standing, I would like to speak with you privately."

Emma cast Steven a nervous, disapproving look.

"Walk with me," Scranius said.

"Well, uh...okay...sure," Steven said, grabbing The Ripper from his bed.

"There is no need for the weapon," Scranius said. "Why must you insist on carrying it about with you?"

"I feel a lot more comfortable if it's close at hand, and even better when it's *in* my hand. This crazy place has taught me to be ready at all times."

Scranius shrugged and said, "As you wish," and motored away.

Steven caught up with the old man and followed him a great distance, past the twelve crosses, and along the row of boulders that lined the border between the river and the Mirror Land.

"I don't like this one little bit," Emma said as Steven and Scranius disappeared from view. "Raven, perhaps you should follow them and keep an eye out from above."

"A splendid idea," Raven said and the big black bird spread his wings and took off.

"Try not to let the old man see you," Emma called out. "And be careful."

"Not to worry," Raven cawed as he soared into the blue. "I will be most cautious in my surveil--"

Suddenly, the bird thudded into an invisible barrier of some sort and was momentarily knocked unconscious. Nina Nita and Emma raced toward him as he began plummeting toward the ground, but fortunately, Raven regained his senses and righted himself.

"What happened?" Nina Nita called out. "Did you forget how to fly?"

"Very funny," Raven said as he cautiously tried several more times to broach the unseen wall, bumping his beak against it. "There is something invisible here that stretches from the ground up and across the sky. It won't let me pass."

"Most suspicious," Emma said. "It would seem that *someone* does not want us to follow Steven and Mr. Scranius Olbaid."

"Indeed that does seem to be the case," Raven said as he alit upon Nina Nita's shoulder.

"I wonder who it is?" the bear said, scratching his head.

Chapter 28

Steven Standing followed Scranius Olbaid around a long bend in the river, to where the Mirror Land widened from one hundred feet across to many, many miles in width.   They stood upon a knoll where a vast forest was visible in the distance, and beyond that, the skyline of an enormous, dark city with great buildings whose tops were shrouded in colossal clouds.

"Where are we going?" Steven asked at last.

"I wanted us to have a little privacy away from that meddlesome girl and squawking bird," Scranius said. "Those two are no good for you; they will only drag you down."

"What are you talking about? They're my friends and I care about them."

"Ah, yes, loyalty," Scranius said. "That is one of your many admirable qualities, but in this case, your loyalty is misplaced. Now, the bear, however, has potential. He is a physically strong and imposing figure, and just dim-witted enough to be put to good use."

Steven shook his head. "I can't believe you're talking this way, Mr. Olbaid. I'm really disappointed--"

"No, no, you must understand that I am merely looking out for your own good," Scranius countered. "Trust me. I am far older and wiser than you, and am therefore able to see the big picture much more clearly than you. There are great and wonderful opportunities all around you, young Mr. Standing. You have to be clever enough to take full advantage of them."

"I don't know what opportunities you're talking about," Steven said. "Look, nothing's changed for me...I'm still just trying to get back home. That's all."

"Ah, but you must accept the fact that it is impossible for you to go back there, and make adjustments accordingly. You should take advantage of what I am offering you."

With that, Scranius grabbed Steven's hand and shouted, "Come with me, boy, and I will show you what could be yours."

Leaving the wheelchair far behind, they soared hand in hand for many miles, high above villages and thick forests. Steven cried out in surprise at first, and then with exhilaration as they swept left and right, spinning and weaving at the speed of a rocket. Steven was breathless with wonder when they finally landed on the rocky crest of the tallest mountain overlooking the dark city.

"Wow! How did you do that?" Steven shouted. "That was awesome!" Then he realized that Scranius was standing on the peak with him. "Hey, what about your wheelchair? I didn't think, I mean, I just assumed you couldn't use your legs."

"Well, let's just say we are 'in the spirit' right now," Scranius said with a crooked grin. "And, as you must know, anything is possible in the spirit realm."

Scranius spread his arms wide with a grand gesture, and the heavy clouds fled from the sky, revealing the lofty tops of the silver skyscrapers. "That is the City of Nis. More striking than anything you saw in The After, is it not? That's because my creations are more impressive than anything Big Father can make."

"*Your* creations? Are you saying you built that city?"

Scranius smiled once again in his crooked way. "All that you see before you belongs to me. I rule this city, I rule the Angry Forest, and I rule the Mirror Land. Soon the Ooljee shall be mine, as well. And after that, the After City itself will be under my control."

Steven's eyes were wide and he was shaken by the drastic change in the little old man he'd known. Thinking him to be delusional, Steven said, "Maybe you're not thinking clearly right now. I know you have some magic powers, but do you really think you own all of those places?"

"I am more powerful than you can imagine," Scranius said quite matter-of-factly. "And I am giving you the opportunity to make something of your After-life. I could use a strong, bright young man as the Captain of my Legions. Surely you want to be on the winning side in the ultimate battle of the Universe."

Steven's head was spinning as he tried to make sense of what he was hearing.

Scranius continued, "If you choose wisely, you can have everything your heart desires – riches, fame, girls, power, possessions. Wouldn't you like to have all the pizza you could eat, anytime, anywhere? Wouldn't you like to be the star player in my Mirror Land Baseball League and have the crowds idolize you and fall down at your feet? Just say the word and all this can be yours."

Steven studied the old man and wondered how dangerous he might be, and how much truth, if any, there could be in what he was saying. The words of Alexia came back to Steven; he could hear her speak them in the back of his mind: *There is a time to be clever and a time to stand and fight; know the difference.*

"Wow, when you put it like that, it really does sound incredible," Steven said. He spoke slowly and carefully, but his mind was racing in search of a plan, hoping to buy himself some time. "But it's just so much to take in all at once. I'd have to give up on my dream of getting back to my old life...and seeing my parents again, you know. That's a big step. Can I at least think about it for a little while?"

Scranius Olbaid studied Steven for a long moment, and nodded. "Alright, then, I will permit you to sleep on it, but then I will expect your answer. And I warn you that if you refuse my offer...I will be forced to make...*other arrangements*."

There was something in the way the old man spoke those last two words that sent a chill through Steven. It sounded like a thinly veiled threat, and it made Steven wonder what terrible things this mysterious old man could possibly do to him and his friends. Once again, Steven just wished he could wake up from this nightmare.

Chapter 29

Steven Standing lay on his bed in the darkness and, of course, he could not sleep. It had been nightfall by the time he and Scranius returned to their camp, and Steven had spoken to none of his friends about what transpired on his walk with the old man. Bang was now sitting up on the bed, watching Steven closely.

"What happened out there today with Scranius?" Bang whispered.

"I don't even know where to begin," Steven said. "I don't know if Scranius is delusional or mad or if maybe he's actually telling the truth."

"Well, what did he say?"

"Yes, you must tell us," Emma said, suddenly slipping onto the edge of Steven's bed.

"Jeez, Emma, you scared me," Steven said. "How do you sneak up on people like that?"

"It is a gift," Emma replied. "Now tell us what happened today."

"Hold on a minute," Raven said as he and Nina Nita joined the discussion. "I don't want to miss a word."

"Well, Scranius took me up on top of the highest mountain that overlooked--"

"A mountain top? How did he get up there in his wheelchair?" Emma asked.

"He flew," Steven answered, rattling off his story quickly, excitedly. "He grabbed my arm and took off with me super-fast. It was unbelievable. And he showed me a massive city, bigger than the After City, with a huge river running right through the middle of it. Scranius told me that he ruled all of it, that he rules this whole place. He tried to convince me to stay here with him and help him run things. He wants me to be the Captain of his forces or something like that. He says that since I can never go back to my old life, I should make this my home, and that I can have everything here that I could ever want."

Steven paused and took a breath.

"Did you see any salmon in the river?" Nina Nita asked.

The others gave the big bear an *'Are you kidding?'* look and Raven pecked him on the head.

"Ouch," Nina Nita said. "What did I do wrong? I been craving salmon for a long time, and there aren't any in this river. I looked."

"Can you possibly shut up about food for even one hour?" Raven asked.

The bear scratched his head and thought about it. "Gee, I don't know…a whole hour?"

Emma turned back toward Steven and said, "So, anyway, what did you do? How did you respond to Scranius?"

"I told him I needed to think about it for a little while," Steven said.

"Think about it?" Emma said incredulously. "Surely you are not serious. You cannot trust this man."

"Well, I was so creeped out by him and the whole thing that I was just trying to buy some time," Steven said. "I wanted to get back here and talk it out with you guys."

"Well, the way I see it, we have four options. Let's look at them in a logical and organized manner," Raven said, fluttering his wings and hopping to the center of the bed.

158

"You're the smartest bird I know," Nina Nita said proudly.

"I am likely the only bird you know," Raven said with a smile. "But thank you for the compliment."

"No, you're not," Nina Nita argued. "I knew that bat named Bartholomew."

"But bats are not birds," Raven said.

"They look like birds and they both fly."

"Friends, we need to focus," Bang barked softly.

"Yes, we do," Raven said, gathering himself and beginning again. "Now, back to the subject at hand. As I see it, our first option would be to turn around and go back the way we came."

"No, absolutely not," Steven said adamantly. "I have come this far and I'm not going to turn back now."

"I suspected you would say that," Raven said. "Option number two: you could take Scranius up on his offer, become his Captain and we could all stay here with him."

Steven, Emma, and Bang shook their heads *No* and Nina Nita said, "I don't wanna stay here. That big Zero wall thing makes me nervous. Sometimes I think I see faces in there."

"Okay, option three," Raven continued. "Steven, you could face Scranius in the morning and tell him point blank that your answer is *No*. Then we can see how he reacts and take it from there."

No one said anything for a minute. Finally, Steven asked, "What's option number four?"

"We take the initiative and try to bust through the Zero Line right away, before the old man, or whatever he is, comes back for your answer."

"I think I like the sound of the fourth option best," Steven said. "Because I can't give up now, and I have a feeling Scranius is going to do everything he can to keep me here."

"There is a fifth option," a voice said. "You can all die."

"Where did that come from?" Steven said.

Raven tilted his head and listened intently. "I believe we have a gremlin under the bed. Birds have excellent hearing, you know."

"We know, we know," Nina Nita said. "You keep reminding us."

Just then, a short, stubby creature with long, bony arms slid out from beneath the bed in a flash. It was unlike any animal Steven had even seen – like an upright, pygmy rat with human arms. Raven squawked and feathers flew as the creature grabbed the black bird and slammed him to the ground, rendering him unconscious.

"There! Good riddance," the creature hissed.

Nina Nita tried to stomp or pounce upon the small beast, but it was far too quick and agile. Every time the bear reached for it, the creature slipped away, cackling and giggling maniacally all the while. Back and forth it went, under the bed, over the bed, under the blankets, between the bear's legs, and even hopping on the bear's back at one point.

Quickly Emma pulled a wooden spindle from the footboard of the bed, and chanted:

"Sausage in patty, sausage in link,
Sausage too old surely will stink;
Emma be nimble, Emma be quick,
Give Emma a pygmy stuck on a stick!"

And the spindle flew from her hand like a dart, pierced the foot of the little creature and stuck him fast to the ground.

"Eeeiiiiiyyyaaa!!" the thing shrieked. It looked down at its foot with great surprise; then swiveled its head slowly toward Emma. Its eyes were on fire.

"Uh oh," Nina Nita said. "It looks real mad."

"Don't just stand there," Steven shouted. "Get it now while it's pinned."

But before they could move, the creature transformed right before their eyes, growing into a ten-foot tall pig-man. Snorting and oinking, it snapped the wooden spindle in its foot as though it were a twig. Drool slid from its grungy mouth, and hung in strands that stretched all the way to the ground. The long, sharp tusks of the beast gleamed in the sunlight, and it pointed them toward Emma.

"I do not like you," it snarled. "Never have."

Wielding The Ripper, Steven jumped between them. "What are you supposed to be? King of the pig-men?" he said with false bravado, hoping to sound much more confident that he really was.

"Ah, dear boy," the pig-man said. "Though I do appreciate the compliment, flattery will get you nowhere with me. You see, I am much so much more than king of the pig-men."

Emma pressed close to Steven from behind and whispered in his ear, "I admire your gallantry but I think you should not be so brazen toward this boarish beast."

Steven whispered back, "He's probably used to everyone around him trembling in fear, so I thought I might try a different approach and see what happens."

The pig-man began to laugh. He put his hands on his hips, tipped his head back and laughed as though he'd just heard the world's funniest joke.

"Steven Standing, I like you," the pig-man said. "I have right from the very beginning. I sincerely wish you would join me."

161

"Who are you?" Steven asked. "What are you talking about?"

"Perhaps this will help," the Pig-Man said as he transformed once again, this time into the frail, white-haired man in the wheelchair.

"Scranius?" Steven said. "I don't understand--"

"I wanted you to come over to my side, young Standing," Scranius said. "There is no greater insult, no greater slap in the face that I could have given Big Father than for you to have come over to my side. Just think of it – the 'Mistake that would be the Savior' defecting to the dark side. How glorious that would have been. Do you not see the beauty in my plan?"

"I knew it," Emma said, stepping out from behind Steven. "I knew there was something bad, something wrong about you. You are the Great Serpent, are you not?"

"Let me answer your question in this way," Scranius said. And he transformed yet again, this time into a monstrous snake as long and as wide as a large tree trunk. He opened his mouth to reveal fangs nearly the size of Steven's legs. "Now do you recognize me, you ugly little girl?"

"Leave her alone!" Steven shouted. "It's me you want. Come get me."

"Oh, no, no, no," the Great Serpent said. "You are incorrect. I want both of you. I want you to serve me, and I want the girl to go back into her deep, dark, lonely cave to suffer forever." His face contorted with a twisted, evil grin and he slithered toward them slowly, tauntingly, hoping to milk as much fear from them as possible.

"I hate you!" Emma screamed and spit at the snake.

"Ah, very good," the Great Serpent said. "At least the little brat has spunk. But I've grown weary of her babbling." The snake's tongue shot from its mouth and

162

flicked Emma sharply, knocking her into the rocks by the river, and leaving her unconscious.

"No!" Steven yelled, wielding The Ripper before him threateningly. "Why don't you fight me, you big coward?"

With both Raven and Emma out cold, Nina Nita edged sideways hoping to flank the snake while it was focused on Steven. But the Great Serpent was aware. "Now Mr. Bear, do not be a fool," the snake said. "I have a soft spot in my heart for you and do not wish to harm you, but you are pressing your luck. For your own good, I will cage you up."

The Great Serpent spit a spray of venom into the air, and as it came down, it formed a cage of metal bars around Nina Nita. Enraged, the bear shook the cage with all his might and roared, "You hurt my friends! You're a bad person, a very bad person."

"Ah, you are *so* right about that," the Great Serpent hissed with a twisted smile.

Chapter 30

Steven Standing and Bang stood alone with their backs up against the shimmering Zero Line, facing the Great Serpent. The snake was confident, over-confident, toying with them like a cat with a mouse trapped in a corner.

"Three down and two to go," the Great Serpent said. "Are you feeling lonely?"

"Looks like we need a miracle right about now," Steven whispered to his best friend.

"We've got to find a way to buy some time," Bang said. "Keep him talking."

"Yeah? And then what?"

"I don't know. You'll come up with something."

Steven thought fast. "So, Mr. Serpent, if I join up with you, how will that work exactly? I mean, what would you have me do?"

"Hhmmm, maybe the offer is no longer on the table," said the Great Serpent.

"But you didn't give me enough time to think it over," Steven said. "I was just talking about it with my friends when you showed up."

"You realize, of course, that I have ways to persuade you to serve me, if necessary. If I were to imprison someone you cared about – your dog, for example – I imagine you would gladly do my bidding in order to save his life."

"You don't have to do that," Steven said, continuing to stall, but running out of ideas.

164

"Yes, it is much more satisfying when someone serves willingly rather than being coerced," the Great Serpent said. "Big Father and I both prefer honest devotion to forced labor. But one does what one must, eh?"

"You know, it sure was a lot easier talking to you when you reminded me of my grandfather," Steven said. "I get pretty nervous talking to a giant snake."

"You do realize, of course, that regardless of which form I assume, I am still far superior to you. For form is ultimately irrelevant; you could not defeat me even if I took the form of an ant."

"Sure, I know that," Steven said, humoring the arrogant reptile.

"And why do you insist on brandishing that foolish weapon, young Standing? The puny magic of that stick is no match for me."

"Certainly does a lot more bragging than fighting, doesn't he?" Bang whispered.

"I was thinking the same thing," Steven said. "Maybe it's time I take him by surprise and show my fangs."

Steven had been holding The Ripper out in front in a defensive manner, but now he allowed the bat to droop to the ground, giving the appearance of surrender. He leaned on it casually. "Okay, Scranius...uh, can I still call you Scranius?..."

"Yes, boy, you may address me as Scranius if you wish," the Great Serpent replied. "What is on your mind?"

"Well, I've thought about it," Steven continued. "I see there's really no way for me to get through the Zero Line. It was crazy for me to think I could actually return to The Before, and I sure don't ever want to go back to The After. I hated it there. So I guess it makes sense for me to stay here with you. Will you really let me play baseball for your team?"

165

"My boy, you can be the Captain of the team, as well as the Captain of my Legions, if you show yourself worthy."

"Then I'll join your side and you can even have my lucky bat," Steven said, holding The Ripper out for the snake to take, as a gesture of good will and conciliation. "But if I do this, there's just one thing I ask. Please promise me that you won't hurt my friends any more. Can that be our deal?"

The Great Serpent weaved about slowly, his scaly skin undulating and sparkling as he pondered and studied the young man before him. At last, he spoke, "You have a deal, young Standing. And I am pleased that you are finally beginning to think clearly. As you probably know, I have bartered with many humans throughout the ages and entered into many agreements with them. Rest assured, I always keep my part of the bargain and deliver what I promise."

"I believe you," Steven said.

The snake transformed back into the little old man, smiled his crooked grin, and reached for the bat. "I'll take that now," he said.

The very moment Scranius touched the bat, in that one, single split-second of time when both Steven and the old man were in contact with The Ripper, Steven released all his pent-up fury and power into the bat. It surged like never before and blasted a bolt of energy so powerful that it knocked Scranius back fifty feet and up against a boulder. He crumpled in the dirt, stunned, smoldering and senseless.

"Sorry, I changed my mind," Steven said.

Nina Nita, still imprisoned inside the cage, roared with delight, while Emma regained consciousness, shook out the cobwebs and got to her feet. "Well done, Steven! You did it!" she said, running toward him.

"No, wait," Steven shouted. "Get back to the rocks. I doubt this is over so easily. Go back."

"Too late," Scranius said, slowly getting to his feet. He wasn't smiling now. There was pure, terrifying rage on his face and evil burning in his eyes, but his voice was very low and unnervingly calm as he said, "You ought not to have done that. You will now learn that the twelfth cross, the empty one, was reserved for you all along, Steven Standing."

Scranius reverted to his natural state as the gargantuan reptile known as The Great Serpent, and slithered slowly toward Steven. Emma still stood between the two, facing Steven with her back to the snake

"Point your weapon toward the Serpent," she whispered. "When I signal you, let fire with all your might. Do you understand?"

Steven nodded and directed the Louisville Slugger toward their enemy. "Stay behind me, boy" he whispered to Bang as Emma began to chant:

"Wheat and barley, barley and wheat,
Son of Man with blistered feet..."

Suddenly the Mirror Land began to shake and rumble as though a great earthquake had come upon it, and the ground split down the middle with the wall of the Zero Line on one side and the river on the other.

"Are you causing this?" Steven shouted to Emma.

"No, this is not my doing," she answered.

The ground where Steven, Bang and Emma stood began to tilt slowly, as if to dump them into the crevasse that had opened up in the surface of the Mirror Land. On the opposite side, Raven was still unconscious and Nina Nita remained trapped in the cage of venom. The bear could only watch helplessly as his three friends struggled to keep their footing or to find something to hold onto as they slid ever so slowly toward the gaping hole.

"Do you see what awaits you?" the Great Serpent hissed. "All of creation groans and travails together in pain. Why should you two Mistakes be any different? Two wrongs don't make a right, you know."

From within the dark chasm came the voice of a great multitude, like the wailing of a million tortured souls, and the roar of many waters and mighty thunderings. The Great Serpent opened his mouth wide, jaws unhinged, sharp fangs glistening, tongue shooting out and lashing across the divide.

For a second, just the slightest moment, Steven felt as if all hope might be gone, like he was trapped in some convoluted, bizarro-world version of David and Goliath where the underdog would *not* find a way to overcome, and the giant would ultimately be victorious. Steven shook off the fear and shouted over the din, "Whatever spell you're trying to cast, you'd better make it fast!"

"Just be ready with the bat," Emma reminded Steven, and then continued her chant:

"Trunk of elephant, tail of lizard,
Frozen flame and fiery blizzard;
Now in this, the darkest hour,
Blend White and Yellow all to power;
I give myself for one last spell,
Return this snake to the pits of hell."

"Now!" Emma shouted.

As Steven fired The Ripper, its power somehow channeled through Emma, and her very body seemed to warp and fluctuate as though she was sliding in and out of Time itself. The bat's white-hot energy melded with Emma's Yellow Power, and exploded from her fingertips like a mighty river bursting forth from a crumbling dam. Emma screamed as the resulting explosion sucked her into its center point with twisting ribbons of light and a massive fireball. She and The Great Serpent disappeared, shrieking into the blackness of the bottomless pit.

The force and energy of the blast hurled Steven and Bang backwards into the Zero Line where everything immediately went silent. The last thing Steven heard was Emma's scream; the next thing he heard was his own.

Chapter 31

Steven Standing and Bang tumbled like wet socks in a slow motion dryer, propelled by the mystic might of White and Yellow, yet swallowed up by the pulsating vacuum inside the Zero Line. Steven felt like an astronaut who'd been walking in space, but whose tether had been cut and he was now drifting and spinning head over heels. He knew he was crying out in pain and fear, for he could *see* the actual sound waves of his own voice following him, trying to catch up with him. There was no chance to grieve for or even think about those they'd left behind – Emma, Nina Nita, and Raven.

Bang and Steven were in a world of contradictions – light moving at the speed of sloth, glowing darkness, weeping laughter, wisps of dense matter, phantoms chasing shining orbs, clouds without water, trees without bark, black holes spewing light, and white holes absorbing darkness. Steven could not tell how long they tumbled through the wall – it might have been one minute or it may have been one hundred years – but everything he'd ever known or said or done flashed through his mind and back again.

Finally, it ended just as abruptly as it began. Steven's scream caught up with him and rattled in his ears as he and Bang burst forth from the Zero Line into the realm of the Backwards Lookers. Steven slammed against the opposite wall where he crumpled and promptly wretched upon the floor.

"You're going to have to clean that up," one of the Backwards Lookers said to him, and handed him a mop. "We keep a clean cube here."

Unsteadily, Steven raised himself to his hands and knees and looked around. Oddly enough, the realm of the Backwards Lookers did indeed appear to be a 20 foot by 20 foot by 20 foot cube. It was a gleaming, sparkling white room with bright lights – though Steven could not tell where the light was actually coming from – and it reminded him of an operating room in a hospital or the high-level security laboratory where his father worked. There was a lectern in the center of the room and a cabinet against one wall; nothing else.

The person holding the mop was a short woman with weasel whiskers and tall, bushy strands of hair that stood up high on her head like the branches and leaves of a full tree in summer.

"Hurry, please," the woman said. "We must process you quickly. We have another traveler due in here in approximately nine hundred years."

Steven could not yet find his tongue to speak, so he stood up, obediently took the mop and cleaned up his mess. He handed the mop back to the woman and it promptly disappeared.

The room's other occupant scribbled something on a clipboard he clutched to his chest. He was a tall, Frankenstein-looking sort of fellow with six arms and only one eye, squarely in the center of his forehead, and he chewed incessantly on a No. 2 lead pencil.

"I am the First," the tree-headed woman said.

"The first what?" Steven asked.

"And I am the Second," the one-eyed being said.

Puzzled, Steven simply stared at them.

"My name is First," the woman explained.

"And my name is Second," the man said.

171

Steven nodded slowly and said "Okay, then, good to meet you. I'm Steven Standing."

"Yes, we know who you are," First said. "And you want to return to The Before."

"That's right," Steven said. As exotic as the woman's head was, Steven found himself staring at the eye of the Cyclops creature, Second.

"With one eye comes singleness of mind," Second said to Steven. "One eye and six arms means I focus clearly and accomplish much. Six eyes and one arm would be to see much but do little."

Steven nodded and said, "Cool."

Bang looked askance at Steven and barked softly, "*Cool?*"

"Do you understand the Power of Mystery?" Second asked.

"I'm not sure what you mean."

"So then, if you are not sure of what I mean, does that indicate that you have a working theory of which you are not yet totally convinced? Or, was your response more of a fallback on common vernacular, and did you mean it to indicate that you truly have no idea at all?"

"Um…I'm going to go with…the second one," Steven said.

"Good answer," Bang said sarcastically.

"Who or *what* is this creature?" First asked, looking down on Bang with disdain, and as though she had not noticed the dog before.

"This is my dog, Bang," Steven said.

Second thumbed through a very large, old book on the lectern. "Yes, yes, I see it here," he said. "A domesticated canid, *Canis familiaris*, bred in many varieties…carnivore of the Canidea family having prominent canine teeth and long, slender muzzle, barrel-chested with bushy tail…"

172

"My tail isn't bushy," Bang said under his breath.

First turned to Steven and said, "Why is the dog with you? Only one may enter the Portal at a time. The dog may perhaps come back in nine hundred years--"

"I remind you that appointment is already booked," Second interrupted his partner.

"Ah, yes. That slipped my mind. Well, then, the dog could attempt to schedule the following appointment in 1800 years," First said. Then she turned toward Second with a perplexed look. "Has one of these creatures ever passed through the Portal back to The Before?"

Once again, Second opened the tome and rifled through the pages, flipping them back and forth in search of the desired information. "No, I do not find where such a thing has ever occurred."

"What about my backpack and bat?" Steven asked. "May I take those with me through the Portal. I mean, assuming you allow me to pass through, of course." Steven was trying to be diplomatic and win their favor.

Second read from the book, "The One who passes through the Portal is permitted to take with him his personal belongings – the clothing he wears and only those other things which he can carry."

"Well, then, sir and madam..." Steven began very politely. "According to the official rules, I ask that you permit me to take this dog along with me through the Portal...again, assuming that you permit me to pass."

"On what basis?" First asked.

"First of all, your rulebook states that I may take my personal belongings, and this dog clearly belongs to me."

Bang bristled just a bit.

"Secondly, it says that I may take those belongings which I can carry. And I can easily carry Bang."

The two Backwards Lookers weighed Steven's words silently and carefully. Second chewed on his pencil and reviewed the Rulebook, deep in thought, murmuring, "Hmm...uh huh...mmhh hum..." First twirled one of her strands of twig-like hair and paced back and forth in the small cube. After a few minutes, they put their heads together and whispered.

Finally, First said, "Your point is well taken and we have made our decision. If we grant you passage, you will be permitted to take your possessions with you, including the doggish creature."

"Thank you," Steven said.

Bang grumbled quietly to himself, "Come all this way...go through so much...get stabbed by a scorpion...just to get here and be insulted."

"Sshhh," Steven whispered. "Just play along."

"Now, let us finish the questioning," First said. "Where did you come from?"

"Uh, well, I came from the other side of the Zero Line, the Mirror Land."

"Before that." Second said.

"I came from The After. Is that what you mean?"

"Before that." First said.

Steven answered curtly, "I came from planet Earth – Los Alamos, New Mexico. 107 Center Street. I came from my mom and dad. I came from a long line of Standings. Does any of that answer your question?"

Calmly and softly, First said, "And...before that?"

Steven narrowed his eyes and gritted his teeth. "Look, this is ridiculous. I don't understand what you're talking about."

Bang whispered to Steven with a sarcastic smile, "Just play along, remember?"

"Smart-aleck," Steven said under his breath.

Second rummaged through the pages on his clipboard and frantically scribbled notes.

First said, "Here is your next riddle: You have wood you must chop for the fire. But there are two rabbits in the hole, a fence to mend in the pasture, and one glass of sweet tea on the table. What do you do?"

Steven shook his head and looked skeptically at his inquisitors. First was calmly combing out her hair and Second was again biting nervously on the end of his pencil. Steven looked down at Bang and made wide eyes at him with a shrug.

"Have you changed your mind?" First asked.

"About what?" Steven questioned back.

"About returning to The Before."

"No, of course I haven't changed my mind."

"Then you must answer all the questions to our satisfaction or you will not be permitted to enter the Portal," First warned.

Steven swallowed and said, "Oh. Can you repeat the question, please?"

"You have wood to chop for the fire. But there are two rabbits in the hole, a fence to mend in the pasture, and one glass of sweet tea on the table. What do you do?"

Steven thought for a moment and said, "I chop the wood for the fire."

First nodded approvingly and Second scribbled on his clipboard.

First continued the interrogation. "Can corruption extend even into the Holy of Holies? That is, are there snakes in the Halls of Heaven?"

Steven answered quickly and firmly, "Yes."

Again First nodded approval and Second scribbled.

Feeling a bit cocky, Steven looked at Bang and raised his eyebrows, tilted his head from side to side with a bit of swagger. *I'm really on a roll now.*

First said, "You understand, of course, that in order to return to The Before, you must go back to your moment of Death. Are you prepared to do that?"

A bit of Steven's swagger immediately dissipated. "What? So, you're saying that I really am dead? Like, right now, I'm dead? Seriously?"

Second and First looked astounded. "Why, of course you are dead. You died in The Before, else you would not have gone to The After, and you would not be here now," First said, shaking her head at Second. "Can you believe what they're sending us these days?"

"Okay, okay, I'm dead now. I get it," Steven said, realizing there was no point arguing this point, and hoping to assuage their displeasure with him. "So, do you mean that I will enter back at the point right before I died?"

"No, that is incorrect. I will read the appropriate passage," Second said, turning pages in the Rulebook. "In order to return to the Before, the Returnee must pass back through each and every specific rung on the Ladder of Mortality, including the direct and full re-experience of the Returnee's death."

"Wow, I hadn't thought about any of this," Steven said, looking at Bang. "Pretty creepy, huh?"

"Don't ask me; I'm just a possession."

"Very funny," Steven said.

"What is your answer?" First asked. "Are you prepared to pass back through your death, fully experiencing it once again, but this time exacerbated by the rigors of the backwards cosmic transformation?"

"Will it hurt?" Steven said, trying to joke through the fear.

"Yes, very much," First said.

Steven put on his game face and said, "I've come this far, been through so much…there is *no way* I'm going to quit now. I don't care how much it hurts or how difficult it is. I'm ready."

Chapter 32

Steven Standing and Bang sat on the floor of the cube while First and Second discussed the specifics of the case. As they waited, Steven rubbed his sore shoulder and remembered the wolves that slashed him there. Thoughts of Alexia, Volpe, the Brisbanes, and even Hilda circled in his weary mind as he leaned back and closed his eyes. Steven gripped The Ripper tightly and recalled the many battles he'd fought with his lucky bat, and how he'd freed Emma Free with its mysterious power. He missed her, Raven, and Nina Nita, and hoped they had somehow survived the blast that cast him and Bang across the Zero Line and here to the Backwards Lookers.

They have to let us go through the Portal. I won't take No for an answer.

Steven put an arm around Bang and rubbed his ears. They smiled weakly at each other.

"I know what you're thinking," Bang whispered. "Don't worry...they will say *Yes*."

"I just don't understand what's taking so long," Steven said. "I can't stand this waiting." He stood up and began to pace.

"Sit down, please," Second said, crossing two of his arms across his chest in a parental manner. His third hand held his ever-present clipboard, his fourth held a cup of grapefruit juice, his fifth a gnawed pencil, and his sixth rested on the lectern.

Steven glared at the one-eyed man for a moment; then sat down grumbling to himself.

"You possess the impatience and pigheadedness of youth," Second said.

Steven couldn't help thinking of Raven, and that, if the bird were here, he would make some silly comment about a pig he once knew.

"Yes, he does," First said. "But he also possesses remarkable wisdom and intelligence for such a young boy. He's actually quite extraordinary."

"We must cast our votes now," Second said.

"Yes, it is time," First said.

Each of the Backwards Lookers wrote something on a small white card and handed it to Steven.

Steven held them awkwardly, too nervous to look at them. "What are these for?" he asked.

"Our decisions are on those cards," First said. "Read them aloud. It is required of the applicant to read the cards out loud within the confines of the cube."

Steven swallowed hard. His hands were shaking as he held the first card up. He couldn't find his voice.

"What is written on the card?" Second asked.

Steven's countenance dropped and his voice quivered as he said, "The card says *No*." Steven hung his head and tried to control his disappointment and anger.

"What does the other card say?" Second asked.

Steven was stunned to see the word on the other card. "It says *Yes*," he exclaimed. "That's one *Yes* and one *No*. What does that mean?"

"That means you are granted access to the Portal," First said with a smile.

"But one of you voted against me," Steven said. "I don't understand."

Second read from the Rulebook, "When rendering a decision, if both representatives from the Society of

179

Backwards Lookers vote either in favor of or against the applicant, then the applicant is denied access to the Portal. A unanimous vote, whether positive or negative, is grounds for an immediate rejection. However, if the vote is split, the applicant is granted access to the Portal."

"I don't…I mean, well, thank you. Thank you very much," Steven said. "It just seems weird…do you mean that if both of you had voted in my favor, I would have been denied?"

"Yes, that is correct," Second said.

First explained, "Contrast is everything in our decision-making process. One who seeks to return to The Before must be tender yet tenacious, with a spirit that stirs passions, both positive and negative. A proper equilibrium is what we seek, and a split vote is the perfect indicator of that balance of charm and abrasiveness, darkness and light."

"I think they're saying that you're a good guy who can also be a real pain in the behind," Bang said.

"Yeah, I got that," Steven said.

"Steven Standing, are you now prepared to enter the Portal?" First asked.

Steven stammered a bit, taken aback by the suddenness of it all. "That's it? Isn't there some sort of introduction or training I have to do, like Portal 101 or something?"

"There is nothing we can say to adequately prepare you," First said. "As with all things in Life, this Journey is into the Unknown."

"Be aware that there been a shifting in the universal balance of power of late," Second said. "The timeline's cosmic corridors are redefining and realigning. The Great War of The Before has played a part in this."

"What Great War?" Steven began to ask, but Second raised two of his six arms in a stopping gesture, and said,

"I realize you do not understand much of what we say to you. But store it to your memory, and the day will come when you will remember and understand."

First placed a hand gently on Steven's shoulder and said, "Steven Standing, the sun shall shine upon you, and you will flash upon the Earth in glory for a moment or two or a thousand perhaps. And the light you leave behind will warm and guide others along their way."

Steven didn't know why, but there were suddenly tears in his eyes and he was trembling. Bang leaned close against him offering comfort and support.

First continued, "Prepare yourself for the sorrow and wonder ahead. When your transformation comes, you will jettison all worldly trappings, shell and husk, to deliver the essence of Life unto those you touch."

Steven secured his backpack with The Ripper safely inside, and cradled Bang in his arms. "You've put on weight," Steven said with a little smile. The room was silent for a moment as Steven stood before the lectern.

"Are you afraid?" Bang whispered.

"A little," Steven replied. "Are you?"

"Yes, but only that you'll drop me."

"It is time," First said.

"Okay…I'm ready…but where is the Portal exactly?" Steven asked, looking all around.

"*You* are the Portal," First answered. "And this is the Door to the Portal." She pointed toward one of the cube's walls and it disappeared, leaving only a vast emptiness stretching nowhere and forever.

"Be strong, Steven Standing," Second said. "The Mistake who would become Savior must share and bear the sins and sorrows of many."

Steven looked puzzled. "I don't understand--"

"Fear not. As with all things, simply close your eyes, breathe deeply, and take one step forward," First said. "And may your last day be your best day."

With Bang in his arms, Steven Standing stepped through the open Door, bound for The Before, eager to return home, anxious to see family and friends, and determined to regain his old life.

But things would not, *could not* be as they once were. They never are.

END OF BOOK ONE